Yo.

D0528759

DR. MORELLE MEETS MURDER

Here is another collection of the strange adventures of Doctor Morelle. The sardonic detective's cases include: an hotelier killed with a brass candlestick; a Baroness poisoned with cyanide; a diamond robbery, and the shooting of zoologist Professor Raymond. The doctor, in his inimitable cerebral style, also investigates: a fake suicide; the stabbing of the wealthy Mr Franklyn; the ex-prisoner accused of murder, and the strangled film star. All whilst aided — or handicapped — by his gentle, timorous assistant, Miss Frayle.

ERNEST DUDLEY

DR. MORELLE
MEETS MURDER

LINFORD
Leicester

First published in Great Britain

First Linford Edition
published 2010

British Library CIP Data

Dudley, Ernest.
    Dr. Morelle meets murder.- -
    (Linford mystery library)
    1. Morelle, Doctor (Fictitious character)- -
    Fiction.
    2. Detective and mystery stories, English.
    3. Large type books.
    I. Title II. Series
    823.9′14–dc22

    ISBN 978–1–84782–978–8

Published by
F. A. Thorpe (Publishing)
Anstey, Leicestershire

Set by Words & Graphics Ltd.
Anstey, Leicestershire
Printed and bound in Great Britain by
T. J. International Ltd., Padstow, Cornwall

This book is printed on acid-free paper

1

Dr. Morelle Meets Murder

There is no doubt that Doctor Morelle would have laughed to scorn any suggestion that Miss Frayle was in any way necessary to him in order to carry on his activities in a satisfactory way. Yet the fact remained that since she had left his employ nothing seemed to have gone right at the famous house in Harley Street. As for his present secretary, Miss Grimshaw, she was as disappointing as all the others who had filled the post since Miss Frayle's unfortunate departure.

The work fell behind, he found himself often stumbling for words, and as a result it was necessary to ask Miss Grimshaw to stay late in order that he would be able to deliver the thesis on which he was engaged, with her assistance, for publication in *The International Medical Journal* at the agreed date.

1

On two nights she had agreed to remain after the hours which had been specified for her; on the third night, however, Miss Grimshaw jibbed.

'If you think that I'm going to stop till all hours of the night, every night of the week,' she declared, with a petulant toss of the head, 'you've got another think coming, Doctor Morelle. Look at the time! Twenty past ten, and I've been slaving away since nine o'clock this morning — '

'In point of fact,' he interrupted her suavely, 'you arrived five minutes late.'

She ignored his thrust.

'No wonder,' she retorted, 'that I'm the umpteenth secretary you've had since Miss Frayle left you. And more fool she to stick the job as long as she did! The others wouldn't and I'm not either.'

Doctor Morelle was unable to resist observing:

'Your syntax is becoming somewhat involved.'

'Listen to you!' the other burst out. 'Always ready with some nasty, sneering sarcasm. You're not human, that's your trouble. You're a machine and you expect other people to act like machines, too. Well, I'm not made of clockwork, and I'm sick of being treated as if I were. So goodnight, Doctor Morelle, and goodbye!'

The door slammed loudly and Doctor Morelle sighed.

He lit an inevitable Le Sphinx while he pondered the situation. He had got used to the idiosyncrasies of feminine nature since the departure of Miss Frayle, but this was probably the worst outburst of temper that he had had to endure. With another sigh he unearthed the first batch of notes that needed his attention. Then the bell rang.

'Ah!' he murmured with an air of quiet satisfaction, 'that will be Miss Grimshaw returning to offer me her abject apologies. I suppose under the circumstances I shall have to accede to the plea for reinstatement which she will doubtless be making.'

He did not look up as the study door was pushed open slowly.

'So you have changed your mind in this

little matter of your departure, Miss Grimshaw,' he remarked icily.

'Hello, Doctor Morelle.'

He started up in considerable surprise. This was the last person he had expected.

'Miss Frayle!' he exclaimed.

'Did you think it was someone else?' she asked in what she imagined to be her most appealing manner.

'I — er — I — '

For the first time Miss Frayle could remember, the Doctor was at a loss for a reply. Then he recovered his familiar poise. 'I was expecting Miss Grimshaw, returning to finish her work.'

'I'm so glad you've found someone else who doesn't mind working late hours.'

The Doctor, however, decided to ignore this, and continued:

'I am eager to know to what I owe this unexpected pleasure, Miss Frayle. Sit down.'

Miss Frayle sat down, but offered no explanation of the object of her visit. She had retained a key to the Doctor's front door and, after ringing the bell, had realised suddenly that she could enter.

She found it slightly amusing to be giving him a surprise.

'I was under the impression,' Doctor Morelle was observing, 'that you were happily occupied in your new situation in Cornwall.'

Miss Frayle tittered lightly.

'I've left Mrs. Padmore, the lady I went to when I left you. She's gone to live in Dorset with a widowed sister who has just arrived from Australia.'

Doctor Morelle at once seized, with his customary quick wittedness, on what to him represented the important part of this statement. 'You mean,' he said, 'you've come to ask if you can have your old post back?'

Miss Frayle shook her head firmly. 'Oh, no, no, Doctor!' she exclaimed. 'I'm sure your — Miss Grimshaw, did you say her name was? — I'm sure she's taking care of you very well indeed. No. As a matter of fact I've come to consult you on behalf of a Colonel Vane.'

The Doctor eyed her sharply. 'Proceed, Miss Frayle.'

'His room is next to mine in the private

hotel where I'm staying. I've only been there a few days, and every night I've been awakened by the Colonel crying out suddenly in alarm and then shouting as if he were terrified. Last night his attack seemed to be worse than usual, and I got up. As I opened my bedroom door the noise got less and there, standing very still outside the Colonel's door, was his servant, an Indian called Shan Gopay. He saw me and I asked him what was the matter.'

'This appeals to me considerably, my dear Miss Frayle,' the Doctor said. 'Pray proceed.'

'Shan Gopay looked at me and said he was afraid the Colonel had been disturbing me. I asked if he were ill. He explained it was what he called a 'mind-sickness', which had been troubling the Colonel, bringing on recurrent nightmares and causing him to cry out in the middle of the night.'

'And did you ascertain anything of further interest?'

'As I was talking to the Indian, the Colonel shouted again. It sounded to me like: 'The ruby! My ruby!' And then his voice died away in a moan.'

'Did you question the Indian servant as to the precise significance of the reference to a jewel?' Doctor Morelle asked.

'I said that it sounded as if he were saying something about a ruby, but the Indian replied that ever since Colonel Vane had come back from India a strange shadow had lain over his mind.'

'And why, my dear Miss Frayle, have you formed the opinion that I can do something to help the unfortunate officer?'

'I asked his servant if he could not see a doctor, but Shan Gopay said that nothing could be done. I told him that I knew a very famous doctor — you, Doctor Morelle — who would be able to put him right. The Indian said that he did not think there was any cure for what was preying on his master's mind.'

'Simple case of anxiety neurosis, my dear Miss Frayle,' the Doctor observed. 'It may possibly be linked with the acquisition of the precious stone which he mentioned. As to that, we can ascertain the facts when we have had an opportunity of some conversation with the gentleman concerned. And when do you suggest would be a propitious moment for my seeing him?'

Miss Frayle clasped her hands together in delight. 'Tonight, Doctor? Before he goes to bed. I'm sure that you can stop him from having another of those dreadful nightmares.'

Doctor Morelle was quite accustomed to some measure of admiration, but he was somewhat surprised to learn that Miss Frayle had such touching faith in his medical abilities.

'You are too flattering, Miss Frayle,' he said smoothly. 'However, since it appears to be a fact that your own slumber is jeopardised by Colonel Vane's sufferings, I am naturally all the more anxious to give due consideration to the case forthwith.'

'Oh, Doctor Morelle! I've been all day wondering if I dared to bother you — '

'Let us proceed at once upon our double errand of mercy,' the Doctor continued, completely ignoring her remarks. 'We will endeavour to obtain a taxi.'

The taxi secured, Miss Frayle gave the

necessary instructions, and it was only a few minutes before they arrived at the Clevedon Private Hotel.

'It's only quite a small hotel, of course,' Miss Frayle said apologetically, as she fumbled in her handbag for the key. 'And they lock up rather early. I left my key behind once, and I had a fearful job banging away at the door before Mrs. Holt, the proprietor's wife, let me in.'

Doctor Morelle stood by with ill-concealed impatience while Miss Frayle laughed and chatted. She produced the key and succeeded in opening the door.

As the door opened, however, the Doctor suddenly gripped Miss Frayle's arm.

'Miss Frayle,' he murmured. 'Can you hear anything?'

An agitated female voice was exclaiming: 'Who's that? Who's there?'

'A lady in a state of considerable psychological agitation,' the Doctor went on. 'Can you give me any clue as to her identity, Miss Frayle?'

'That is Mrs. Holt, the proprietor's wife,' Miss Frayle said in some surprise, and then shouted: 'It's me — I mean 'I' Mrs. Holt — Miss Frayle.'

Mrs. Holt, a middle-aged woman with greying hair, who had once been pretty but who had now lost all pretence to good looks, came into the hall where Doctor Morelle and Miss Frayle were standing. Her face was a study of acute anxiety.

'Oh, my husband! My husband!' she exclaimed.

Miss Frayle looked considerably alarmed. 'Mr. Holt?' she asked. 'What has happened?'

'He's dead!' Mrs. Holt exclaimed. 'Murdered!'

'Murdered?' Miss Frayle repeated the word in a hushed whisper, which was a sufficient indication of her alarm.

'In here,' gulped Mrs. Holt in a voice that was not far removed from hysteria. 'In the office. And they've robbed the safe.' Her voice trailed away.

'Perhaps if I might intrude,' Doctor Morelle said. He had listened to Mrs. Holt's remarks with close attention and now brought himself to her notice.

'Oh yes,' said Miss Frayle, suddenly

remembering his presence which the rush of events had completely driven out of her mind. 'This is Doctor Morelle. He was coming to see Colonel — '

Mrs. Holt broke in. 'A doctor? Thank heavens! Will you come in here at once, Doctor, though I'm afraid there is nothing much you can do.'

She led the way into the little office off the hotel lobby and the Doctor followed her, Miss Frayle on his heels. 'Try to calm yourself,' he said. 'I'll endeavour to ascertain the extent of your husband's injuries.'

He saw at once, however, that the man's wife had not been mistaken. The base of the skull was shattered. Clearly he had been struck a heavy blow with some massive object.

'No doubt,' he said to Mrs. Holt, 'your husband was struck down with this heavy brass candlestick on the desk?'

'Yes, Doctor,' she agreed. 'I kicked against it when I came into the room.'

Dr. Morelle glanced at her sharply. 'When *did* you discover your husband?' he asked

'No more than five minutes ago.' Mrs. Holt was wringing her hands in despair. 'Oh, it was horrible, horrible!'

The Doctor was never impressed by exhibitions of emotion. He brought the conversation right back to earth. 'Where were you when your husband was attacked?'

'He and I were playing cards in our sitting room. He said that he could hear someone in the office. I thought it was one of the guests and didn't realise anything was wrong until about ten minutes had passed and he didn't come back.'

'No one else,' Doctor Morelle queried, 'was here when you entered?'

Mrs. Holt shook her head. 'I came straight in, the light was on — and saw him. I didn't know what to do — '

Her voice petered away into a shuddering moan.

'Then Miss Frayle and I arrived, is it not so?'

'Yes. I was just going to 'phone for a doctor.'

Doctor Morelle, during the latter part

of this conversation, had been looking around him with keen interest, studying everything that was in the room.

'You say,' he remarked quietly, 'that the safe had been disturbed?'

'Yes. There should be money in it, and some valuables belonging to some of the guests.'

The Doctor walked across to the safe. 'Obviously,' he murmured to himself, 'the safe has been opened by use of the combination. It has not been forced. The thief or thieves entered and escaped by this window. The lower half is open.'

The Doctor had been speaking his thoughts aloud. Mrs. Holt overheard at least the latter part of them,

'The window must have been forced,' she said. 'My husband was always especially careful to lock it up at night.'

Miss Frayle now showed signs of distinct agitation. She moved to Doctor Morelle's side and gripped his arm tightly.

'Do you wish to attract my attention, Miss Frayle?' he asked acidly.

'Listen!' she hissed. 'Someone is coming.'

Footsteps approached. Then the door opened quietly and a dark-skinned man entered noiselessly.

Miss Frayle said, in a voice that was almost a scream: 'Mr. Gopay!'

The Indian looked around him, saying:

'I am so sorry if I am intruding.' He broke off suddenly with a gasp, and added: 'Mr. Holt! Whatever has happened to the poor gentleman?'

Doctor Morelle, looking carefully at the Indian's face, replied:

'He's dead.' Then, sharply turning to Miss Frayle, he added: 'Quick, Miss Frayle! I think Mrs. Holt is fainting.'

Indeed, Mrs. Holt seemed to be in a bad way. She was swaying on her feet and appeared likely at any moment to collapse in a heap on the floor.

'I think that it would be as well to take her to the sitting room. Place her in a recumbent position and administer a little water. That should be sufficient to produce satisfactory results.'

Miss Frayle led the fainting woman from the room and Doctor Morelle, dismissing the matter from his mind, turned to the Indian.

'You are the Doctor, yes?' the coloured man said.

'I am Doctor Morelle. You, I presume, are Shan Gopay, Colonel Vane's servant?'

'That is correct.' The Indian looked at the Doctor with interest. 'That candlestick which you are examining,' he said, 'did that kill the unfortunate gentleman?'

'Undoubtedly. Traces of blood and several hairs adhering to the base of the candlestick indubitably indicate where it struck against the skull. There are, however, no fingerprints whatever, which seems to suggest gloves, or that the candlestick was carefully cleaned after the crime had been committed.'

The Indian stood by, impassive, while the Doctor described his own theory of what had happened. Now, however, Doctor Morelle turned to him.

'What attracted you downstairs?'

'I heard Mrs. Holt crying out. I thought that something might perhaps be wrong.'

'Who else,' the Doctor next asked, 'apart from yourself, Colonel Vane, and

Miss Frayle at present resides in this hotel?'

The Indian showed white teeth in a sudden smile. 'One person only,' he said. 'He is a gentleman named Foster. He went out just after dinner and I have not heard him return.'

Then it seemed that the Indian suddenly caught sight of the safe. He held up his expressive hands in horror.

'Doctor!' he exclaimed. 'The safe, it is open! It has been robbed! My master's dreadful dream has come true! His ruby, it has gone! It was in the safe.'

Doctor Morelle looked remarkably sceptical — a not unusual expression for him — but at this moment much more obviously so than was generally the case.

'You are suggesting,' he said, 'that Colonel Vane dreamed that tonight's tragedy might be about to happen?'

The Indian looked thoughtful. 'He has had bad nightmares lately,' he said. 'He often cried aloud about the jewel — that something terrible would happen in connection with it. Though when he wakes he usually cannot remember exactly what it is that has disturbed his sleep.'

There was a cry from some room on the floor above.

'Listen! That is the Colonel now! He went early to his room in order to rest. He must have fallen asleep. I must go to him and see if I can help.'

Doctor Morelle eyed the other for a moment. 'You would be well advised,' he said, 'not to acquaint him with what has occurred here. By tomorrow it is possible that the precious jewel of which he thinks so much may well have been recovered.'

The Indian glanced sharply at the Doctor. It was as if he found it difficult to believe that Doctor Morelle could possibly promise anything so inherently unlikely as the recovery of the Colonel's ruby. Then he said, turning back in the doorway:

'Very well, Doctor. I will preserve silence on the matter. As you say, the gods may yet prove kind and restore his ruby to him.'

Doctor Morelle smiled grimly to himself. 'You mean', he murmured quietly, 'that *I* shall be able to perform that particular trick.'

It was still possible to hear incoherent cries from Colonel Vane, and the Doctor strode swiftly to the door, calling after the Indian: 'I will come up to him presently and administer a sedative which will ensure him a peaceful sleep.'

Then he turned his attention back to the more immediately urgent problem of Mr. and Mrs. Holt. 'Curious,' he mused, 'that the Colonel should exhibit in dreams a foreknowledge of tonight's events. Extremely interesting.'

He glanced swiftly around the room as if to photograph its every detail in his retentive mind. Then he stepped silently into the sitting room where he saw Mrs. Holt, now in full possession of her sense once more, on a couch. Beside her was the still somewhat anxious Miss Frayle.

'Ah, Mrs. Holt,' the Doctor said, 'I am pleased to note that you appear considerably better.'

'She *is* a little better,' Miss Frayle said.

The Doctor appeared pleased at this. 'In that event, Mrs. Holt,' he said, 'perhaps you would try to answer one or two questions which I should like to put to you.'

'I'll do my best,' she promised.

'Are you aware of the combination which opens the safe in the office?'

'Yes.'

'Does anyone else possess this knowledge, apart from your husband and yourself?' was the next question posed by the Doctor. The answer was what he had anticipated.

'Definitely no one else,' Mrs. Holt said. 'My husband would never have dreamed of giving it away. It was known only to him and to myself — and he changed it very often. It was never written down. We used to memorise it.'

'You are sure it could have been known to no third party at all?'

'Quite certain.'

'And did you know anything about the valuables which were kept in the safe — valuables, for the most part, deposited by the guests of the hotel?'

Mrs. Holt looked puzzled at the line of questioning which Doctor Morelle had taken.

'I knew something of what was hidden in the safe, yes,' she agreed. 'But not necessarily the details, or the particular items which might be left there by particular guests.'

'I understand, Mrs. Holt. Did you — if I may be so bold as to cite a particular example — know that the safe contained a precious stone which Colonel Vane had entrusted for safety to the care of your husband?'

There was a slight look of confusion in Mrs. Holt's face as if she were still not at all sure whither this cross-examination was leading.

'Yes,' she said at length. 'I knew that there was something important of the colonel's there. But I did not know exactly what it was, or that it was in any special way valuable.'

Suddenly Doctor Morelle grasped Miss Frayle's arm. A tipsy voice was heard in the entrance hall of the hotel. A man was loudly singing some quite incomprehensible ditty, which was brought to a sudden stop by a loud hiccough. Miss Frayle felt an almost irresistible desire to giggle, which, however, she managed to suppress by a great effort of will.

The man's footsteps passed the door of the sitting room in which they were situated and then unsteadily made their way to the main staircase of the hotel.

'Is that another of your guests, Mrs. Holt?' Doctor Morelle enquired.

Mrs. Holt nodded. 'Mr. Foster,' she said.

'He certainly sounds a little — er — well — ' Miss Frayle searched vainly for the word that would express in sufficiently polite terms the precise state of inebriation in which Foster had apparently come home.

'Just so, my dear Miss Frayle,' said the Doctor in irritable tones. 'And now I think that it is time for the police to take over the case. Miss Frayle, perhaps you would be so kind as to get into telephonic communication with Scotland Yard. I daresay that you can still recollect the number?'

'Whitehall 1212,' Miss Frayle said proudly and promptly.

'What an excellent memory you possess,' Doctor Morelle said. 'Yes, I fancy that I shall, as usual, be able to offer them the information which will lead them directly to the apprehension of the criminal responsible.'

'Doctor Morelle!' Miss Frayle exclaimed, 'do you mean you know who murdered Mr. Holt?'

Doctor Morelle looked at her with that mixture of dislike and irritation that she knew so well from past days.

'I mean,' he said slowly, 'that I know a certain person is withholding the real truth about the murder — doubtless in order to shield either themselves or someone else. Moreover — and this is no doubt what will most interest the gentlemen from Scotland Yard — I know who that certain person is!'

* * *

About an hour later Doctor Morelle, and a somewhat chastened Miss Frayle, were seated in the study. As he smoked an inevitable Le Sphinx, the Doctor was airing his views on the case that he had so neatly elucidated, while Miss Frayle sipped a cup of tea and listened to what he had to say.

'I don't know how you do it, Doctor Morelle. It astonishes me more every time I think of it,' she said.

He smiled sardonically. 'Of course,' he said, 'certain important aspects of the crime immediately presented themselves to me as soon as I entered the hotel. My mental processes will possibly be well known to you by now, Miss Frayle, and were I in the position of dictating a further chapter for inclusion in a future edition of my casebook . . .'

He paused and glanced at Miss Frayle. She pushed her glasses back on to her nose and looked meekly at him.

'There's a notebook here, Doctor,' she said with a hint of a suppressed giggle. 'If you are sure the efficient Miss Grimshaw wouldn't mind, I'd be only too delighted to jot down a few notes for you while the case is fresh in your mind. I know how much importance you attach to not waiting too long before you commit the facts to paper — especially when it has been a difficult and complicated case like this one.'

'This case has been neither difficult nor complicated,' he said in irritated tones. 'On the contrary, it has been extremely simple and straightforward from the start. However, I am inclined to accept your kind offer, since I feel that this is a case which deserves to be put on record if only because it exemplifies the fact that the average criminal invariably neglects to remember some quite vital point — a point which the alert investigator, if he uses his mental powers to the utmost, can invariably notice.'

Miss Frayle was sitting, pencil poised above the notebook, regarding him intently.

'You don't want all this included in your notes of the case, do you, Doctor?' she queried.

Doctor Morelle looked at her suspiciously. Did he detect a note of sarcasm in her voice? Then he said:

'No. Begin here, Miss Frayle: It was immediately apparent to me that, if the safe had been opened by someone without any prior knowledge of the combination, it must have yielded only to the most delicate manipulation of the sensitive mechanism — a feat that only an expert safe-breaker could have performed — or would, for that matter, have attempted. Alternatively, however — ' He broke off suddenly. 'I trust that I am not going too rapidly for you, Miss Frayle?'

Miss Frayle laughed. 'Oh, not at all. This is really great fun. Just like old times!'

The Doctor resumed.

'Alternatively, however,' he went on, 'Holt or his wife could have imparted the secret of the safe combination to someone else. But this seemed a totally impossible suggestion, unless *she* herself had robbed the safe, or passed on the secret of the combination to some accomplice whom her husband had later surprised in the act of the robbery.'

'Quite so,' Miss Frayle agreed.

'I wish you would not interrupt my train of thought, Miss Frayle!' the Doctor exclaimed. 'Resume your shorthand hieroglyphics, please: Considering the extreme force with which the man had been struck down, I was inclined to take the latter view and to consider that some male accomplice of Mrs. Holt had robbed the safe and, being surprised in the act by Holt, had struck him with the brass candlestick which he saw on the table in the office.'

He paused, as if collecting his thoughts for a final paragraph, which would place the whole matter in perspective.

'As we are now aware,' he went on, 'my theory proved correct. The wife implicated Foster, the man whom we heard simulating inebriety as he returned to the hotel . . . '

During the latter part of this piece of dictation, Miss Frayle had shown signs of increasing excitement. She had dropped her pencil, much to Doctor Morelle's irritation since he had to stop dictation while she hunted on the floor for it. Now she burst in with the query that had been hovering at the back of her mind for some minutes past.

'But how,' she asked, 'did Mrs. Holt give herself away to you in the first case?'

Doctor Morelle frowned portentously. 'That, my dear Miss Frayle, I should have thought was obvious enough to the meanest intelligence,' he said.

'Perhaps you will explain?' Miss Frayle asked in her sweetest tones.

'Very well.' With a sigh of resignation Doctor Morelle went on. 'And it might perhaps be as well to include this also in your shorthand notes of the case,' he said. 'You will recall my reference to the heavy candlestick, which was on the desk in the hotel office?'

Miss Frayle nodded quickly.

'Mrs. Holt declared that she had kicked her foot against it when she had entered the office,' the Doctor continued. 'It had therefore presumably been on the floor. She also stated that no other person had been present between her finding her husband and our arrival on the scene. Therefore she must have picked up the candlestick and placed it on the desk herself. I trust that you can follow the line of my argument up to this point, Miss Frayle?'

'Perfectly,' Miss Frayle remarked with considerable satisfaction.

'Good. You will also recall that when I subsequently examined it to confirm that it was the actual weapon with which the crime had been committed, I found that it bore no fingerprints whatsoever. Mrs. Holt was not, of course, wearing gloves — she had not been out of doors the whole evening — and the only question to be settled was who had cleaned the fingerprints off the candlestick, and why?'

'I think I see,' Miss Frayle murmured.

'Pray let me finish my logical construction!' Doctor Morelle snapped. 'The answer was obvious enough. Mrs. Holt or someone else must have removed the fingerprints — because the candlestick bore the imprint of that other person's fingers as well as her own! That other person was, in fact, the murderer. When once I had reached that point, the remainder was abundantly clear.'

Miss Frayle sat up in her chair, eyes wide open with admiration. Her spectacles slipped forward on her nose and she pushed them back with a gesture that Doctor Morelle found irritatingly familiar.

'How perfectly marvellous of you to have worked all that out!' she exclaimed.

'I am quite sure that if I had thought about it for an age, I should never — '

The Doctor held up a commanding hand.

'Purely a ratiocinative process,' he snapped. 'When once the central fact had been grasped, the remainder followed logically and inevitably. And,' he added, '*do* refrain from goggling at me through your spectacles in that way! You know how irritating I have always found your astigmatic — ' He broke off suddenly. He had forgotten that Miss Frayle was by way of being merely a volunteer on this occasion. 'I — I beg your pardon, my dear Miss Frayle,' he said. 'For a moment I thought that you — er — were back — '

Miss Frayle laughed outright.

'Doctor Morelle, it was wonderful!' she exclaimed. 'Just like old times! And when Miss Grimshaw comes back — well, I shall feel quite lost to be away from this study!'

'Miss Grimshaw — er Miss Grimshaw — ' And for the first time in his long career, Doctor Morelle seemed completely at a loss for words.

2

Death of a Baroness

Among his wide circle of acquaintances, there are many who have been known on occasion to deny that Doctor Morelle possesses any human characteristics. According to these people, the Doctor is a soulless machine who churns out scientific hypotheses and the solutions to criminological riddles with unfailing regularity.

Whatever notions of this nature Miss Frayle may have entertained, she appeared to have changed them since she willingly agreed to carry on for a short while as the Doctor's secretary and amanuensis. She was slightly hopeful that she might, in thus reentering Doctor Morelle's employ — even though it was merely a temporary arrangement — be once again taking part in an exciting piece of investigation.

The first day she entered the familiar

study, however, she was slightly disappointed when he announced that he wanted her assistance in putting in their final shape accounts of some past cases. Cases that had occurred when she had been his permanent secretary.

Doctor Morelle's preliminary observations were, however, interrupted by the imperative ring of the telephone bell.

Miss Frayle lifted the receiver. 'Doctor Morelle's house.' And then: 'Oh dear, oh dear! I'll tell the Doctor at once. Just hold on a moment, will you, please? It's Green's Hotel, Doctor Morelle,' she said.

'I have a slight knowledge of that small, exclusive Mayfair hostelry,' the Doctor admitted.

'One of their guests is the Baroness Beauville,' Miss Frayle went on.

'Ah, yes. That no doubt is why, by a piece of unconscious ratiocination, the name of the hotel seemed familiar to me. I have been attending the Baroness for some time past. She has always visited me here and I have therefore never had occasion to go to the hotel where she sojourns during her visits to London.'

'They're afraid she is dead,' Miss Frayle added nervously. 'And they want to know if you will come round right away.'

'Certainly I will,' Doctor Morelle agreed readily enough. 'There was nothing in her condition to lead one to anticipate speedy demise. A slight tachicardia, if I recall aright, but nothing in any way dangerous. Let us go to Green's Hotel without undue delay, Miss Frayle.'

They emerged into Harley Street in the spring sunshine and, by dint of a wave of his famous swordstick and a fierce glare, the Doctor persuaded a taxi to stop. In a few minutes they were talking to the manager of Green's Hotel.

'I think we should go straight away up to the Baroness's suite, don't you, Doctor?' he said.

They made their way to the lift, which swiftly bore them away from the some-what ornate entrance hall of the hotel, up to the second floor.

As they ascended, the manager said: 'It was the new floor-waiter on the second floor, Doctor, who made the sad discovery. He went into the Baroness Beauville's suite by some stupid mistake and found — '

'What time was that?' Doctor Morelle snapped.

'About a quarter past eight,' the manager said. He broke off to glance at the highly polished panelled interior of the lift and glare at the lift-man. 'The panelling is very badly scratched, isn't it?' he remarked.

'Yes, sir,' the lift-man said in apologetic tones. 'Lady Porlock's poodle, sir.'

'Too bad,' murmured the manager, and turned to the Doctor and Miss Frayle once again. 'I'm sorry,' he said, 'but the sight of those scratches distracted me somewhat. I was saying that the floor-waiter made the dreadful discovery at about quarter-past eight. I went up to her suite immediately, of course, but there was absolutely nothing that I could do. She had obviously been dead for some considerable time. Heart failure, I suppose.'

'Poor thing,' Miss Frayle remarked

sympathetically, her comment drowned by the sound of the lift-doors opening. They had arrived at the second floor, where the suite occupied by the Baroness was situated.

As they walked down the corridor towards the entrance of the suite Doctor Morelle glanced towards the hotel manager.

'Have you informed the deceased lady's companion of what has taken place?' he asked. 'She was a Mademoiselle — her name, I fear, has for the moment eluded me in some unaccountable fashion.'

'Mademoiselle Sarlou, Doctor,' said Miss Frayle helpfully. She had, in the past, made several appointments for the Baroness to visit the Doctor in Harley Street. But it was strange that, for once in a while, Miss Frayle's memory for names should prove more reliable than his own. Doctor Morelle swiftly dismissed this thought from his mind, though he made a note that he must ascertain if Miss Frayle were taking some course of mental training. If so, he mused, it might well be that the course would bear investigation, since anything that could improve the mental ability of Miss Frayle would be in some respects valuable.

The manager was saying: 'I 'phoned her at her flat at once. I think that she will be here at any moment now.'

They had now arrived at the door to the suite occupied by the Baroness, and the manager produced a key from his pocket.

'Naturally,' he explained, 'I had the door locked when the tragedy became known,'

'Naturally,' Doctor Morelle agreed. But Miss Frayle thought that there was a somewhat absent-minded ring about his voice.

They walked into the suite and glanced around them.

'The bedroom is through here,' the manager said, leading the way, with Doctor Morelle close on his heels, and Miss Frayle following,

'The Baroness,' he added, in hushed tones, 'was found exactly as you see her now.'

Miss Frayle put her hands over her

eyes, as if she wished to shut out the sight. The Doctor, on the other hand, took in the whole scene at a glance. His eyes flashed from one corner to another, taking in the crimson velvet curtains and the rich carpet, and the tragic figure of the Baroness, so suddenly overtaken by death.

'H-mm.' He leaned momentarily over the prostrate figure of the Baroness Beauville. 'All the external characteristics of cyanide poisoning appear to be present,' he announced, in level tones.

'Poisoning!' the manager exclaimed, horrified. He seemed suddenly to realise how the Baroness Beauville's death might react on the reputation and future prosperity of his hotel.

'No doubt,' the Doctor went on, ignoring the exclamation, 'it was taken in this half-empty glass of orange juice, which I perceive on the bedside table. Nothing whatever in the room has been touched, I presume?'

'Nothing. The waiter came in by mistake, as I said, and as soon as he had realised what had happened he at once hurried downstairs to report the matter to me,' the manager explained. 'But — poisoning! Honestly, Doctor, I am completely at a loss to understand it.'

Doctor Morelle was not impressed by the other's muttering.

'So far as I am able to ascertain from the cursory examination which is all I have as yet been able to perform,' he said, watching the manager closely as he spoke, 'it is highly probable that the Baroness Beauville committed suicide.'

The manager started as if he had been shot.

'Suicide! Suicide? But — this is terrible, terrible! What will people think? What will happen to the hotel and its future? It is a dreadful affair, dreadful, dreadful!'

'Anyone would imagine,' said the Doctor in icy tones, 'that you had taken mercury cyanide yourself. Pray consider the matter in something approaching its correct perspective. Do realize that there are things in this world other than hotels, and that in any case it is the duty of all law-abiding citizens, when a violent and unexpected death takes place, to do everything in their power to elucidate whatever mysterious circumstances may be found to exist.'

The manager looked slightly indignant. No doubt he regarded this as to some measure an assault on his dignity; but he was not able to reply at once, as the telephone rang suddenly and shrilly, thus causing Miss Frayle to jump violently. She thought that there was something uncanny in the telephone ringing in a dead woman's room, and she remarked as much.

'Do not be intolerably sentimental, my dear Miss Frayle.' The Doctor remarked irritably. 'Telephones continue operating whether people are dead or not. I will answer it.'

He strode across the room and picked up the receiver.

'Is that the Baroness Beaville's suite?' asked the voice at the other end of the line.

'It is.'

'Her nine o'clock call, please.'

'I see. Thank you.'

'What was it?' Miss Frayle asked hopefully.

'Merely a routine call,' answered the Doctor. 'Heavy sleepers like to have a telephone call, which will tell them the time in the morning.' He turned to the manager. 'No doubt you forgot to countermand the request that the Baroness should be called at nine o' clock.'

'It was undoubtedly overlooked, in all the worries of the morning,' the manager admitted. 'And in any case, I cannot say that I was aware of any such request having been made.'

For the first time since his arrival Doctor Morelle smiled. 'I did not expect that you would have any such knowledge. After all, one does not expect the manager of a hotel to have within his personal grasp every tiny detail of its organisation. Naturally you would trust such matters to subordinates.'

They slowly emerged into the sitting room again, Miss Frayle hurriedly scuttling ahead as if she were only too eager to get away from the atmosphere of death that had, for her, been so oppressive.

'But what makes you think that she committed suicide Doctor?' she asked. 'Isn't it just possible that it might be an accident, after all? Or, perhaps . . . ? Or perhaps . . . ?' She paused as if aghast at the thought that had sprung unbidden to her mind.

'This French novel,' Doctor Morelle explained in tones which seemed to indicate that he was maintaining a hold on his patience only with the greatest of difficulty, 'lay open on the table of this room as we came in. When I looked around the room it was the first thing that impressed me. Two sentences have been heavily underlined in pencil, and they may, presumably, be considered as containing her farewell message to the world.'

'What two sentences?' asked Miss Frayle eagerly

'If you would kindly give me the opportunity of reading them aloud, my dear Miss Frayle,' the Doctor snapped, 'you would be able to appreciate at its due worth the case which I am at present fruitlessly endeavouring to put before you for your consideration.'

'I'm so sorry, Doctor.' And it really seemed on this occasion as if Miss Frayle were genuinely contrite.

Picking up the book, Doctor Morelle read from it, aloud.

"Et maintenant la derniere des mes bons amis est partíe. La vie est vide, je reste seule tristement šeul.'

Miss Frayle perked up at this.

' 'And now,' ' she said briskly, ' 'the last of my good friends has departed. Life is empty. Only I remain — sadly alone.' '

Doctor Morelle grinned a mirthless grin. 'Brilliant piece of translation, my dear Miss Frayle! How *should* I manage without your able assistance, which is so ever-ready at my side?'

Fortunately for Miss Frayle, who was wondering whether she would survive another verbal attack from the Doctor's sarcastic tongue, the outer door now opened and a young woman, dressed in plain, but obviously expensive, clothes, burst suddenly into the room.

'Oh, my poor friend!' the newcomer exclaimed. 'Oh, what is wrong with the poor Baroness. How did she — ?'

The manager gently grasped her arm. 'Mademoiselle Sarlou,' he said very gently, 'the Doctor here thinks that it is probable that the Baroness took her own life.'

Doctor Morelle was watching Mademoiselle Sarlou's face very closely at this moment. It was not clear to Miss Frayle what he expected to see there but, whatever it was, she thought that he would be disappointed.

Miss Frayle anticipated horror, agitation, even distress. But Mademoiselle Sarlou's face remained almost expressionless.

'I feared that something of the sort might be about to happen,' the Frenchwoman admitted sadly, speaking in calm, even tones, and with a touch of a fascinating accent. 'She had been terribly depressed these past few days — since she received the news of her brother's sudden death in America. He was her last surviving relative, and she constantly spoke of being terribly alone in the world.'

'Poor thing!' Miss Frayle's natural sympathy overflowed into this remark.

'I tried very hard to persuade her to send for you, Doctor,' Mademoiselle Sarlou went on, after a glance in Miss Frayle's direction, 'but she would not allow me to do so. You know she always made a point of the fact that she must not bother anyone more than was absolutely necessary. She felt she was a burden in the world, and she always said that was all the more reason for not letting herself become a burden on too many of the individuals in the world. She had become almost a fanatic on that point.'

Miss Frayle agreed. 'Yes,' she said, 'the Baroness always went out of her way to avoid causing anyone the slightest trouble. Quite meticulous about that, she was.'

The Doctor listened to this exchange with ill-concealed impatience. Then, seeing that there was a slight lull in the conversation, he turned to the manager.

'Now that Mademoiselle Sarlou has arrived,' he said, 'I think that I should like . . . '

'Yes, Doctor?' The manager was clearly eager to meet the Doctor's every wish; almost before it was formulated and put into words.

'I'd like to have a word with the floor-waiter. The man who discovered what had happened to the Baroness.'

'Of course,' said the manager briskly. 'I'll find the man at once Doctor, and send him straight along to you. He must still be somewhere on this floor, and he will be with you in a matter of minutes, at most.'

While they settled down to wait — something that Miss Frayle always found difficult, though Doctor Morelle invariably bore it with philosophic fortitude — Mademoiselle Sarlou sat down on a settee and passed a shaky hand nervously over her brow.

'I had a strange foreboding when I left the poor Baroness last night,' she said.

'Indeed?' Doctor Morelle said. 'And at what time did you depart from this suite?'

'Just before she retired to bed. About a quarter to ten. I prepared her orange juice for her as usual, set her alarm clock for nine a.m., also as usual, and I left her settling down to read a novel for a brief time before sleep.'

'From which she chose her epitaph,' said Miss Frayle with a touch of that melodramatic feeling which Doctor Morelle was always inclined to think assorted so oddly with her streak of sentimentality.

'Her epitaph? Where?' This had clearly shaken Mademoiselle Sarlou more than all that had gone before, since the painful moment when she had first entered the room.

'This underlined passage,' Doctor Morelle said, handling the book with care and passing it over to her.

She read: ' "Et maintenant la derniere des mes bons amis est partie . . . ' The rest of the extract from the book was lost in her sobs, as she sank back in the settee in deep distress. Miss Frayle seated herself beside the distraught Frenchwomen and did her best to administer comfort.

Gradually the sobs subsided. Mademoiselle Sarlou produced a tiny handkerchief, and dabbed, somewhat ineffectually at her eyes. Then she looked up at Doctor Morelle with a smile which was at once apologetic and explanatory.

'She was such a good friend to me,' she said.

'I am sure she was,' Miss Frayle agreed impulsively. 'And that is all the more reason why you should help Doctor Morelle, for he will be able to solve the mystery of the reason why she should commit suicide in this extraordinary way.'

'Do you think he can?' Mademoiselle Sarlou seemed to find it impossible to believe that this should be so.

Doctor Morelle, clearly thinking this was a pure emotional orgy, which would have to be brought to an end as soon as possible, interjected a hasty question.

'Would this be the alarm clock that you set to go off at nine this morning?' he asked, pointing to a neat little chromium-plated clock, which stood on the sideboard.

'Of course,' Mademoiselle Sarlou said readily enough. 'And why do you ask?'

'It stopped,' the Doctor pointed out, at precisely ten thirty-three last night. It therefore failed to ring at the set time of nine-o'clock this morning.'

Mademoiselle Sarlou looked startled at this revelation. 'But that is extraordinary,' she said. 'It has never gone wrong before, and the Baroness has used it for years — ever since I first met her, in fact.'

Miss Frayle, still sitting on the settee alongside the Frenchwoman, now sat bolt upright. It was obvious to the Doctor that she had suddenly been possessed by something that was comparatively rare in her existence — an original idea with bearings on the case.

'Doctor!' she exclaimed.

'Yes, Miss Frayle?'

'What time did the Baroness die last night, did you say?'

'I did not say, as it happens, but I should hazard that death supervened somewhere between ten-thirty and eleven o'clock last night. As you will know from past experiences, Miss Frayle, it is rarely possible to settle with any exactitude the time of death in cases where — '

Miss Frayle, almost for the first time in her career, interrupted the Doctor. She held up her hand with a gesture that was almost commanding.

'Then the Baroness died,' she said in a voice which was full of significance, 'at about the same time the alarm clock in her room stopped!'

Doctor Morelle found this merely irritating. 'Possibly the coincidence has its bizarre aspects, Miss Frayle,' he admitted, 'but I am of the opinion that it is a coincidence to which no real significance may be attached.'

Miss Frayle looked considerably crestfallen. But before she could think of a suitably crushing reply, there was a discreet tap at the outer door.

'Come in,' said the Doctor, and the door slowly opened. The man who came in was clearly a waiter, quite apart from the fact that he was wearing the approved uniform of his office.

'You wanted to see me, sir?'

'Oh, I didn't see you come in!' Miss Frayle exclaimed, rather startled. She had been so deep in her consideration of the coincidence of the clock that she had not even noticed his tap at the door.

Doctor Morelle, on the other hand,

judged that her exclamation was unworthy of any comment.

'You are the waiter who first discovered the deceased lady?' he asked.

The waiter agreed. ''Course,' he added, 'I never knew it was Baroness Beauville then. I thought it was someone else, and when I — '

'How did you come to make such an error?' Doctor Morelle interrupted him.

'Well, you see,' the waiter said confidentially, 'I've only just started in this job and I wasn't sure of who was in which room. I was supposed to take her breakfast into Lady Porlock. She — '

'She has a poodle,' Miss Frayle suggested helpfully, remembering the conversation with the manager in the lift.

'That's right, Miss, she has,' the man agreed. 'Sloppy-looking black thing, it is, what is a terrible nuisance in a hotel, scratching the paint off everything and all.'

'We are not in the least concerned with the habits of Lady Porlock's poodle,' put in Doctor Morelle with some irritation.

'Oh, no, sir,' the waiter said hastily.

'Well, as I was saying, I got her suite mixed up with this one, and that's all there is to it, really. When I comes in here and finds her dead — the Baroness, that is — I thinks that it's Lady Porlock. See? And so I goes right down to the manager's office, and I reports to him that Lady Porlock is dead, but when he comes up he finds that it's not Lady Porlock at all, but the Baroness. That is, if you follow me?'

Doctor Morelle seemed quite satisfied by this explanation. It had, indeed, been lucid enough.

'You have been more than explicit,' the Doctor agreed. 'And now, Miss Frayle, if you have finished administering to Mademoiselle Sarlou in her distress, I think that it would be as well if you would telephone to the police.'

Miss Frayle appeared to be slightly disturbed at this suggestion.

'The police, Doctor?' she queried. 'But — Doctor, oughtn't you to tell the manager first? I mean to say, as it's only a matter of suicide, he may feel that he should have been consulted, and he may like to — '

Doctor Morelle was now truly roused, as Miss Frayle had seldom seem him in her long career as his secretary.

'Miss Frayle,' he snapped, 'your advice is as gratuitous as it is ill-informed. Kindly obey the instructions which I have given you, and when you are in touch with some official at police headquarters, please inform them that I strongly suspect that there is foul play, and not 'only a matter of suicide,' as you so fondly imagine.'

Miss Frayle sprang to her feet, but was suddenly conscious of a moan from the woman beside her. She glanced down at Mademoiselle Sarlou, to see that lady reel and slide slowly towards the floor.

'Oh, dear,' Miss Frayle murmured, grasping Mademoiselle Sarlou's senseless form just in time to stop her from collapsing in a heap. 'What shall I do, Doctor? Mademoiselle Sarlou has fainted.'

'Attend to her, if you will,' Doctor Morelle said. 'I'll attend to the telephone for once, since you are incapacitated from doing so.'

He grasped the receiver firmly, told the

girl on the hotel switchboard: 'Whitehall 1212 at once,' and then waited.

The waiter had listened to all this in what seemed to be a state of daze.

'Foul play, eh?' he now remarked.

'That,' Doctor Morelle agreed almost amiably, 'is what I suspect, not without good grounds, to be the case.'

The waiter took alarm. He did not know Doctor Morelle, and he may have thought that what the Doctor considered to be a friendly, confident smile, was in, actuality a grin of considerable menace. At any rate he said, suddenly: 'Here, you needn't look at me like that!'

Doctor Morelle ignored this, still awaiting Scotland Yard on the 'phone.

The waiter slowly came towards him, fists clenching as he approached.

'I told you, didn't I,' he said, 'that I know nothing about it? Why, if you think that you're going to pin a murder on me, you're mistaken, and I can tell you that I — '

'Stand back!' Doctor Morelle warned him, still grasping the telephone receiver with his left hand, and his right hand on the handle of his slim walking stick.

Still the waiter advanced, his fists ready for a fight. But then, quite suddenly, the Doctor touched the handle of his stick, there was a quick movement — and the slim, rapier-like blade of his swordstick emerged.

'Blimey!' exclaimed the waiter, falling back aghast, his hands descending limply to his sides. 'A blinking swordstick, is it?'

The door opened slowly and the manager came in. 'Gracious me!' he exclaimed in alarm. 'What on earth is going on here? What has happened, Doctor Morelle?'

The waiter spoke sullenly. 'The Doctor thinks that the Baroness was murdered, sir,' he said.

'What! Murdered? Doctor Morelle?' the manager gulped.

'He starts accusing me of having killed the old lady,' the man said grimly. 'And I told him that I wouldn't stand for it. I knew nothing about her, and I — '

'No one,' Doctor Morelle said quietly, 'has yet been accused of any crime, though doubtless, when the police come to investigate the matter, they will.'

'But what makes you think that the

Baroness met her death in any such way?' asked the manager. Doctor Morelle silenced him with a wave of his hand. His 'phone call had come through.

'Scotland Yard?' he asked. 'This is Doctor Morelle. Could you kindly send someone at once to Green's Hotel? I think it is a case of murder.'

* * *

'And how, precisely, do you think that I should end that chapter in my book, Miss Frayle?' the Doctor asked. It was some time later, and they had returned to the study at the house in Harley Street.

'By saying what happened afterwards, and what Scotland Yard discovered to be true,' she suggested.

'An admirable suggestion,' he said. 'Well, you may resume your dictation at this point. It was in fact a case of murder. Under subsequent police interrogation Mademoiselle Sarlou confessed that she had administered cyanide in the orange juice. Leaving after her victim had retired to bed, she underlined the farewell passage in the novel in order to convey the impression of suicide.'

Miss Frayle looked thoughtful. 'I still think,' she said, 'it was unfair of you to expect me to suspect something was wrong merely because of that 'phone call, which was to awaken her at nine o'clock. After all, the alarm clock had gone wrong.'

For a moment Doctor Morelle spluttered irritably. 'Anyone but a, half-witted — ' Then he resumed, more suavely: 'That is, my dear Miss Frayle, if I may explain?'

'Please do.'

'Mademoiselle Sarlou declared that she had set the alarm as usual for nine o'clock the following morning. The clock, how-ever, stopped at ten thirty-three that night. Surely the morning telephone call was at once significant? The Baroness had obviously observed the timepiece stop when it did so, and had thereupon requested the hotel switchboard to wake her by telephone instead. That is a request she would never have made if she were at that moment contemplating suicide. Remember the poison was cyanide, a poison that is extremely difficult to procure, and if suicide had been the true explanation it would have had to be premeditated. The motive for the crime was that Mademoiselle Sarlou had learned of the Baroness's intention to cut her out of her will.'

Miss Frayle drew a neat line at the end of the notes that she had been taking. 'Will that be all, Doctor?' she asked.

'I think so,' he replied. The telephone rang. 'Except for answering that, Miss Frayle.'

'Hello,' Miss Frayle said. 'Miss Carstairs, is it? Yes. Better late than never! Tomorrow morning. Ten o'clock. Very well, Miss Carstairs. Goodbye.'

She slammed down the receiver triumphantly and said to the Doctor: 'And I know that you will be able to deduce what that call meant?'

'Simple,' he replied. 'You've just made an appointment for me to see a new patient.'

'Not a new patient,' Miss Frayle said. 'A new secretary!' And she was out of the door before he could answer.

3

The Disappearing Diamonds

Doctor Morelle appeared somewhat perturbed as he sat in his study and regarded the telephone. Once or twice he made as if to lift the receiver only to let his hand fall, as if he found the call that he had to make infinitely distasteful. At last, however, he made up his mind, gripped the receiver firmly and rapidly dialled a number.

'Is that Miss Frayle?' he asked presently.

'Why, yes. Surely that isn't Doctor Morelle?' came the familiar tones at the other end of the line.

'It is I, Miss Frayle.'

The Doctor hesitated and then continued: 'I'm afraid that the secretary I was expecting decided after all against taking up the position. It is all most inconvenient for me, as I have a lot of work that is requiring attention at once. I — er — telephoned to ask you if you — er — that is, I was wondering — ' He paused, betraying a certain lack of his usual resolution.

'Do you know, Doctor,' Miss Frayle replied, still with a suspicion of amusement in her voice, 'if I didn't remember how stupid I used to be when I was your secretary, I'd almost suspect you of deliberately scaring off applicants for the post. Just so that you would have the opportunity of offering me my old job back once again.'

The Doctor spluttered violently. This was almost too much for his equilibrium.

'Did you say something, Doctor?' Miss Frayle asked.

'My dear Miss Frayle,' Doctor Morelle was regaining his normal composure with a great effort of will. 'My dear Miss Frayle, believe me I should welcome your return to Harley Street wholeheartedly.'

Miss Frayle laughed quietly. 'I'll look in again this morning — just once more — to give you some temporary help until you can get someone more satisfactory for a permanent secretary, shall I?'

'Please do,' the Doctor responded.

'I can't come at once,' she explained, 'as I have to go to the hairdresser's to make an appointment; but I'll be with you in a few minutes.'

'Goodbye until then, Miss Frayle,' the Doctor said, in tones which in anyone else would have been considered tones of gratitude.

'Goodbye. See you soon,' Miss Frayle replied, and rang off.

The Doctor sat for some time deep in thought. No one had ever been able to solve the mystery of his feelings towards Miss Frayle, but there could be little doubt that he was extremely pleased now that he knew she would be once more assisting him, as in the past.

He pondered these matters for awhile, and then set about arranging some papers which lay on the desk before him. When Miss Frayle arrived she would have to be set to work at once, and his material must be ready, so that he could start dictating without any undue delay.

The 'phone rang, and he picked up the

receiver in a nonchalant manner.

'Doctor Morelle's residence.'

'It's me — I mean, it's 'I'!' was the agitated response.

'Where are you?' the Doctor snapped. 'I was expecting you to be here by this time.'

'I thought you might be pleased to talk to me again,' Miss Frayle interposed suavely. 'But, of course, if you find me as irritating as all that — ' She left the rest to his imagination.

Doctor Morelle quickly recalled she was, in fact, conferring upon him a considerable service by coming to his aid where others had failed him. Forthwith he presented a side of his nature that most people would have been amazed to know that he possessed.

'I should have said I was wondering what had detained you, Miss Frayle,' he said, almost apologetically.

'I'm at the hairdresser's now,' Miss Frayle exclaimed. Her voice quivered with excitement as she went on quickly. 'Can you come round at once? A man's been robbed, and he's in rather a state about it.'

'Really, Miss Frayle!' the Doctor protested. 'You cannot expect me to be at the beck and call of every victim of any petty robbery which may eventuate. You had better tell the man that the best solution of his problem is to send for the police. They will be able to do as much for him as I should, since the detection of robbers is more in their province than it is in mine.'

Miss Frayle openly scoffed at this advice.

'I wouldn't call stealing ten thousand pounds' worth of diamonds a petty robbery!' she added: 'I shan't be able to help you, I'm afraid, for thinking and worrying about the poor man all day. In fact, I'm not at all sure that I shall be able to come along as I promised and help you, unless — '

Doctor Morelle was not one to stick too rigidly to his own point of view when he saw that his own immediate interests were threatened.

He said, quickly: 'Naturally, my dear Miss Frayle, I don't wish you to have to endure a moment's mental suffering. I know its effect on a person of your acute sensibilities. So if there is anything which I can do, I will do it.'

'It's not very far from you, actually,' Miss Frayle explained. 'It's in Lewis Street, just off Bond Street, Oxford Street end. Vernon's the name. Vernon, ladies' and gentlemen's hairdressers.'

'Very well, Miss Frayle, I will be with you as quickly as a taxi-cab will bring me.'

And he was as good as his word. Within five minutes he was talking to Miss Frayle and a very perturbed Mr. Woods in the quietude of a back room at Messrs. Vernon's shop. Mr. Woods was a plump man of middle age. His normally cheerful countenance was overshadowed by anxiety.

'It so happened,' Miss Frayle explained, 'that I was just leaving, Doctor, when Mr. Woods came rushing out.'

'Nearly knocked her over, I did, Doctor,' Woods said. 'Of course, I was much too late. The thief had disappeared long before that.' There was a rueful tone in his voice as he said this. 'In fact, I was so upset that I nearly fainted. Silly of me,

I suppose, but you can guess how I felt at that moment.'

'It was not a bit silly of you, Mr. Woods,' commented Miss Frayle with her customary sympathy. 'It must have been a ghastly shock for you.'

The Doctor, however, showed not the slightest inclination to waste his precious time in expressions of sympathy.

'Tell me,' he said, 'how was it that you came to have such an extremely valuable collection of precious stones in your possession?'

'I'm employed by Crane and Sayers, the diamond dealers of Hatton Garden,' the other explained. 'I was taking these diamonds along to Mrs. Vallance's home. She lives in Park Street, not far from here.'

'I see.' Doctor Morelle nodded gravely.

'She had in mind a necklace which her husband had offered to get made for her birthday. It was to be an extra-special affair, made to an exact design, which she fancied. And as I came out of our office in Hatton Garden, to bring the stones along, one of the chaps said to me that I could do with a haircut, especially as I was on my way to call on such a posh customer. He was joking, you see. But I'd allowed myself plenty of time, and as I was cutting through Lewis Street here to Park Street, I noticed this shop, and — well — I thought that there was something in what the chap had said. I thought it would take only a few minutes to have a trim, and so in I popped.'

Doctor Morelle considered this information in silence for a few moments. Then he said: 'You entered straight from the street into that saloon which I can see across the passage there?'

'Yes,' chirped Miss Frayle brightly and helpfully, 'the ladies' department is upstairs.'

'Thank you, Miss Frayle!' the Doctor said quietly. 'That dark, sallow, individual shaving a customer over in the saloon — is he the proprietor?'

'Can't quite tell from here,' Woods remarked.

'That is Mr. Vernon,' Miss Frayle interjected. 'You need new specs, Mr. Wood. I can see him well enough from here with my glasses, you know.'

'Can't see a thing without mine,' admitted Woods. 'Anyhow, Mr. Vernon has been very kind to me, letting me rest in his office like this, when I had had such a shock.'

Miss Frayle's sympathy once again came to the fore.

'Yes, you were very upset,' she said.

Doctor Morelle had been carefully studying the general layout of the premises while this discussion had been going on. Now he appeared to have come to some conclusion. He swung round, facing Woods again.

'The door by which you entered would appear to be the only way in or out of the gentlemen's saloon?'

'Yes, it is,' Mr. Woods agreed. 'I hung up my overcoat with the case of diamonds in the inside pocket — a big one, as you can — and got into the chair.'

'You found one chair unoccupied when you entered?' Doctor Morelle queried.

'Mr. Vernon's. The other chair was occupied by a fat, red-faced man, I remember. The assistant was just finishing cutting this man's hair as I came in, and he went out a few minutes later, long before my trim had been done.'

'I notice,' Doctor Morelle pursued, obviously carrying out a train of thought which Miss Frayle was totally unable to follow, 'that there are only two barber's chairs in the saloon.'

'It was while I was having a shampoo — after the trim — that another young fellow came in. He looked around the shop for a minute, said he was expecting to find a friend, who hadn't turned up, and then went out again.'

Doctor Morelle again paused, in order to digest this new piece of information.

'You suspect that he took the gems with him?' he asked.

'I'm afraid that there's no doubt at all on that point,' Woods explained. 'He stood beside the coat-stand quite long enough to take the jewel-case out, and a few minutes later, when I went to put on my coat, the case had vanished.'

Miss Frayle looked impressed at this reconstruction of the way in which the robbery had presumably taken place.

'Do you think,' she asked, 'that he had followed you from Hatton Garden, and that he saw you come into this shop?'

Woods looked a trifle worried at this suggestion. 'I couldn't say, Miss,' he admitted. 'It's possible, of course. Or he may have done it on the spur of the moment, without even knowing what was in the case.'

Doctor Morelle was clearly not impressed by Miss Frayle's attempt at detection. He turned to Woods again. 'You have not yet advised your firm of this unfortunate occurrence?' he asked.

Woods shook his head. 'Frankly,' he said, 'I don't quite know what I'm going to tell 'em. There will be big trouble over this business, of course. After all, I was responsible for the diamonds while they were in my possession. And then this young lady here said, Doctor, that you might somehow be able to get the jewels back without anybody being told anything about it, and so I thought I'd just wait and see what you would be able to do.'

Doctor Morelle showed a strange trace of modesty. 'I fear,' he said, 'that Miss

Frayle is inclined to claim for me powers which I am not always entirely able to live up to.'

Miss Frayle tittered gently. 'Doctor,' she said, 'you know you never fail!'

Doctor Morelle smiled. 'It is gratifying, my dear Miss Frayle,' he said, 'to learn that you repose such amazing trust in my abilities, though I am afraid that it is at the same time something of a responsibility.'

He walked towards the door as he spoke, and Miss Frayle looked very surprised at this move.

'Where are you going, Doctor Morelle?' she asked.

'I have the intention,' the Doctor explained, 'of carrying out a little experiment which might possibly lead to interesting results. While I enact the role of the suspected person, entering and quitting the saloon, I should like you to remain here, in this office, observing through the window the reactions of both the proprietor and his assistant.'

The door of the office had a large glass window in it, and through this Miss

Frayle and Mr. Woods were able to watch Dr. Morelle's actions.

'Can't see what he'll find out by doing this,' Woods said.

Miss Frayle was almost indignant at the implied criticism of her employer in Woods' remark.

'Doctor Morelle would not be doing anything without some definite purpose, you may be sure, Mr. Woods,' she said. 'You'd be very surprised if you knew the things he spots just by hitting on something very simple — but something which nobody else has noticed. It's his power of observation combined with his brilliant brain which enables him to do these things — things that would be absolutely impossible for anyone else.'

'You're a sort of friend of his, I suppose?' Woods said, watching her intently.

'I used to be his secretary,' Miss Frayle explained. 'At the moment I'm just helping him out, because he is busy and his new secretary hasn't turned up yet.'

'Oh, I see,' Woods remarked. 'Not engaged to him or anything like that, then?'

Miss Frayle blushed rosily at this suggestion.

'Good gracious, no!' she stuttered, conscious of the blush suffusing her countenance. 'Whatever made you think that anything of that sort could be true?'

'The way you was praising him up to me,' Woods explained. 'Sorry, I'm sure, if what I said embarrassed you, Miss.'

'Not in the least embarrassed,' Miss Frayle said airily, though the still remaining traces of the blush gave the lie to what she was saying. 'It was such a completely fantastic idea, that was all. That was why it so took me by surprise.'

They stood in silence and watched Doctor Morelle, now in the men's hairdressing saloon. Mr. Vernon was shaving a man, and the assistant was sitting down, reading a newspaper. As the Doctor came into the room they both looked up, and noticed that he moved over towards the hat stand. The proprietor and the assistant both looked at him, and then he went over and spoke to the assistant — obviously asking him a question.

'No doubt,' Miss Frayle said, as if she found it necessary to explain to Woods the way in which the Doctor set to work on these occasions, 'he will be bringing that assistant in here to ask him a few questions about what was going on.'

'Don't think he'll be much help to us,' said Woods with a supercilious sniff.

'He might be able to give us some idea of what the thief looked like,' suggested Miss Frayle.

'I could do that,' said Woods. 'I should know him again any time I saw him.'

Before Woods could give Miss Frayle any further information on this point, however, Doctor Morelle came back, followed by the assistant, a sallow youth.

'My client had just gone,' the assistant was saying as they approached, 'and I was reading the paper when the chap you're talking about came in.'

'Was there anything particularly striking about him?' asked the Doctor.

The man hesitated, as if he found it difficult to reply to a question of this kind.

'I should perhaps amend that question

slightly,' Doctor Morelle said. 'Was there any particular feature about him which struck your eye?'

Again the man hesitated. 'Not as I recall, sir,' he admitted slowly. 'I just give him a casual once-over, folding me paper and thinking that he would soon be taking my chair. But all he says is to mutter somethink about his pal who he was going to meet not turning up. So he just turned around and tootled off. That's about all I can tell you, I'm afraid, sir. You see, I didn't know that anybody would be asking questions about him after, and I had no special reason to pay any attention to what he looked like.'

Here Woods burst in. 'I saw the blighter all right!' he exclaimed. 'I could see him in the mirror, you understand. He was a thin-faced chap, with a little moustache, with a scar on the left-hand side of his face. He was wearing a light-grey trilby.'

The assistant partially confirmed this description.

'Yes; I remember that he was wearing a light-coloured hat,' he agreed. 'As I said, I was pretty well occupied with the paper,

I'm afraid. You see, I was wondering whether it would be worth having half-a-dollar each way on Pretty Lass for the two o'clock, or whether the second favourite wouldn't be a better bet. And when you're concentrating on something of that sort, sir, you don't pay very much attention to somebody who just tootles in and tootles out again, like the fellow what we've been talking about.'

Doctor Morelle nodded and appeared even more thoughtful after this exchange of opinions. Miss Frayle, studying his countenance, thought that she had seldom seen him so obviously a prey to conflicting ideas. Indeed, she was for a moment almost of the opinion that he had been defeated by the problem that was awaiting solution. Soon, however, his expression cleared, and Miss Frayle felt a twinge of suppressed excitement, for she was sure that he had, somehow, managed to see his way through the problem, and that the solution would now very soon be divulged.

'Perhaps,' the Doctor said, speaking to the hairdresser's assistant, 'you would kindly ask your employer to step in here for a moment? I see that the customer to whom he was attending has been dealt with, and is now on the point of leaving the saloon.'

'Certainly, sir,' the assistant said. 'I'll go and tell him.'

The assistant walked to the door, opened it, and made his way to the saloon.

Swiftly the Doctor turned to Miss Frayle.

'I crave your assistance, if you would be so kind as to give it to me, Miss Frayle,' he said.

'I should be only too pleased,' she said, with an almost arch expression on her face.

'I should like to know what was the result of your vigilance while I was reenacting the entrance of the mysterious customer in the saloon,' the Doctor explained.

'Nothing very startling, I'm afraid,' Miss Frayle said. 'I noticed that when you appeared in the room both Mr. Vernon and his assistant looked up at you. But they only glanced for a moment or so, and then they went on with what they had been doing before. It did not seem to me that they paid much attention to you.'

Doctor Morelle looked considerably gratified at these remarks from his temporary secretary.

'Excellent, my dear Miss Frayle!' he exclaimed. 'That is precisely what I had hoped you would say. Your observations amply confirm my own opinion that neither of them glimpsed the suspected person for more than a moment. In other words they did not see enough of him to identify him in any reliable manner. They were too absorbed in their task to pay much attention to the newcomer.'

'Hush, Doctor!' Miss Frayle warned him. 'Mr. Vernon is just coming in.'

Mr. Vernon was of foreign extraction, and there was a slightly excitable air about him.

'Doctor,' he said as he entered the office, 'I understand that you wished to ask me something in connection with this so unfortunate business?'

'I should be very much obliged, Mr.

Vernon,' answered the Doctor, 'if you could give me your impression of the way in which the suspected thief entered your saloon and left it again.'

'He come in. He go out. Poof! Like that. I am much too busy shampooing this gentleman — ' he indicated Woods — 'to notice much about him.'

'Would you know him if you saw him again, Mr. Vernon?' asked Doctor Morelle.

'I think not. I scarcely saw him. As I said, I was much too busy to pay any attention to what was happening. To shampoo properly is to concentrate, you understand.'

'I understand,' the Doctor said, and looked extremely thoughtful once again.

'*I* saw him,' Woods said again. 'He came in just as I lifted my head from the basin. It was a lucky thing that I looked up just then. I got a good look at him in the mirror, you see.'

Doctor Morelle spoke very patiently. 'I know that, Mr. Woods,' he said urbanely. 'But surely it should be clear to you that in a case of this sort it is necessary to get ample confirmation of vital evidence, if it be at all possible. If a man can be identified by two witnesses, the police will be far more impressed than if only a single person is able to identify him.'

'I see.' Woods subsided.

Miss Frayle grabbed the Doctor's arm at this moment. 'Doctor! Look!' she exclaimed. 'Mr. Vernon! Your assistant! He's thrown off his apron and grabbed his hat!'

Doctor Morelle, though interested, was unperturbed by this unexpected development.

'He appears to be effecting a reasonably hasty departure,' the Doctor mused.

Vernon was extremely annoyed, however. He pushed past Doctor Morelle with a hasty 'Excuse me, I must stop him,' and raced quickly into the saloon.

'The thief's accomplice!' Miss Frayle stammered. 'That's what he is! He has realised you've tumbled to his secret, Doctor, and so he's trying to make a getaway.'

Woods, in his turn, was excited by what was going on. He swiftly turned to Doctor Morelle.

'You're not going to let him get away with it, are you, Doctor?' he asked. 'Call the police. That's the thing to do in a case like this. Why, it's quite likely that the chap could lead us to the diamonds!'

Doctor Morelle stood firm. He was like a rock against which all this emotional upset beat in vain. He spoke, calmly and quietly.

'I already have a fairly good notion as to where the missing gems may shortly be located,' he said. 'And personally, I cannot help feeling somewhat sympathetic towards the young man who is doubtless at this moment hurrying on his way amidst the traffic of Bond Street.'

'Doctor!' exclaimed Miss Frayle in considerable surprise. 'I've never known you say that you were genuinely sorry for anybody before!'

The Doctor raised his eyebrows interrogatively. 'No, Miss Frayle?' he said. 'Can it be that, without even my realising it, the influence of your presence is beginning to have a mellowing effect upon my doubtless mordant character? Do you think that it is possible?'

Woods had stood by with ill-concealed impatience.

'Look here Doctor,' he said, 'what about doing something?'

'Doing something?' Doctor Morelle seemed to be puzzled by this demand.

'What about setting the police after that chap?'

'Very well if you insist,' the Doctor agreed. 'Miss Frayle, I should be very much obliged if you would kindly oblige me with your usual efficiency.'

'I know, Doctor Morelle, I know,' said Miss Frayle. 'That old Whitehall 1212 once again!'

* * *

Two hours later Miss Frayle was sitting in the familiar chair in the Doctor's study. The Doctor himself had lit a Le Sphinx and he reclined in his chair and blew smoke-rings gently towards the ceiling and watched Miss Frayle trying to sort out some notes on the desk.

'Do you want to get the affair of the stolen diamonds written down for your

Casebook tonight, Doctor?' she asked.

'I do not know that any such procedure is in any way essential, Miss Frayle.'

'But there is an old saying, never put off till tomorrow what you can do today,' she reminded him.

'Old sayings are not necessarily wise because of their antiquity, you know, Miss Frayle,' he remarked sapiently. 'And in any event, I feel that a case as simple as this one scarcely needs recording in such a formal manner.'

'Simple?' Miss Frayle was incredulous. 'Did you say a case as simple as this one, Doctor?'

'Undeniably it was one of the simplest affairs which I have ever been called upon to investigate, my dear Miss Frayle,' he remarked with some unction.

'*I* thought that it was very difficult and complicated. I still can't make up my mind how you came to decide that the hairdresser's assistant had nothing to do with the robbery. When he ran away I was quite certain that he was either the thief or the thief's accomplice. I should like to know,' she added, 'just why he did that.'

'It was merely foolish panic that drove him to his precipitous flight,' the Doctor explained. 'He thought that events seemed to point in his direction. And in the distant past he had served a brief spell of imprisonment. Like so many people who have been in prison, he thought the authorities would be prepared, in the inelegant phrase of the day, to 'frame him' for a crime of which he was wholly innocent. Hence his desire to leave the shop when he found that he was being questioned as to the happenings of which he had been a witness.'

'I see,' said Miss Frayle thoughtfully. 'But I still think that he was very silly. The police might easily have arrested him as an accomplice.'

'The police would undoubtedly have arrested him as an accomplice,' Doctor Morelle said, 'had I not been able to put them on the track of the actual criminal — Woods.'

'But how did you spot that it was Mr. Woods who had got the diamonds?' Miss Frayle asked eagerly. 'And that the man who popped in and out of the hairdresser's was just acting as a sort of decoy, to make it look as if the jewels had been stolen from Mr. Woods' pocket?'

'Miss Frayle,' Doctor Morelle said quietly. 'Would you answer me a question about a more personal aspect of your life?'

She goggled at him for a moment. Then:

'Why, of course. But I can't see what — '

'Do you, when you wash your hair, continue to wear your spectacles?'

Miss Frayle looked astonished. She was not quite sure what she had been expecting, but certainly not this question.

'Of course not,' she said. 'I have to take them off. Otherwise they would either fall off or they would get so wet that I shouldn't be able to see through them.'

'Precisely.' Doctor Morelle puffed gently at his cigarette and blew another ring of smoke.

'But I still don't see,' Miss Frayle objected.

'Woods was undergoing a shampoo.

Therefore he must have removed his glasses. He revealed earlier on that he was very short-sighted, yet, when the individual whom we were expected to consider to be the thief entered for a brief moment only, Woods was apparently able to describe his features in the most minute detail.'

'I understand,' Miss Frayle nodded vehemently.

'He raised his head from the washbasin,' Doctor Morelle concluded, 'and claimed that in that moment he was able to recognise the face of the supposed thief in the mirror. It was perfectly clear to me that he was lying, and that therefore he himself was the guilty person. Indeed, he had deposited the jewels in a safe spot before coming into the hairdresser's shop. He knew that he might be summarily dismissed from his position with the firm in Hatton Garden, but with such a valuable set of diamonds in his possession, that did not worry him.'

'And all that business of the little scar, the moustache, the thin face, were all nonsense!' Miss Frayle exclaimed.

'All intended merely to confuse the police in their investigations, and we may be sure that when the accomplice is apprehended, as he doubtless will be ere long, his appearance will be completely different.'

Miss Frayle smiled. The Doctor glared.

'What may be the meaning of that self-conscious smirk which is spreading across your countenance?' he asked.

'I was only thinking of something that Mr. Woods said to me, while you were out of the office,' Miss Frayle remarked, the smile still on her face.

'Something of a derogatory nature concerning myself?' Doctor Morelle asked the intonation seeming to indicate that he found this almost impossible to imagine. 'Or was it that he indulged in some sickening piece of flattery with regard to yourself, Miss Frayle?'

'Anyone would think that you were jealous,' Miss Frayle said but the Doctor's reply was to stalk out of the study.

4

The Hampsted Mystery

Doctor Morelle is reputed to have declared that secretaries are the most fickle of animal species. In fact, he has, it is said, roughed out a thesis on the subject of the psychological conditioning that is necessary in order that a secretary may be especially suited for the job that it is intended she should perform. Possibly the fact that he was attempting to put this thesis into effect partially accounts for the difficulty he had encountered in getting a new secretary who would stay with him for any length of time. On the other hand, it may have been due to the fact that his own enormous appetite for work made him keep his secretaries working all hours, seven days a week.

However on one point there can be but little doubt. He had been totally unable to find anyone who would take over the post left vacant by Miss Frayle. He was therefore pleased (though, with his customary reserve, he did not display this pleasure in any ostentatious way) at the fact that Miss Frayle had volunteered to help him out temporarily, pending the arrival of a new amanuensis.

'Are you ready, Miss Frayle?' he was asking somewhat querulously one afternoon, having sorted out some notes from which a scientific paper was in due course expected to emerge.

'Yes, Doctor,' Miss Frayle replied, and then looked up at him brightly.

'Do you wish to utter some inane remark before I embark on the dictation which is your ostensible reason for being here this afternoon, Miss Frayle?' he asked, recognising the symptoms

'You know,' she said thoughtfully, 'I've just been thinking, Doctor.'

'Yes?' The suggestion behind this monosyllable was unmistakable. From long experience, however, Miss Frayle was quite impervious to the arrows of the Doctor's sarcastic wit.

'Yes,' she said. 'You seem to be having

such a difficult time getting a new secretary since I left you — I really can't imagine why it is so difficult — '

'The modern young woman,' Doctor Morelle said sententiously, 'is too busily occupied with attending cinema theatres, dance-halls and the like, and with listening to the more inane matters which are inflicted on a long suffering public by the media, that she is not disposed towards employment that involves a certain amount of cerebral activity.'

'Yes, yes,' Miss Frayle hastily agreed. 'Anyhow, it seems to me — that is — well, I don't want to sound too pushing, you know, Doctor, but — ' Her voice petered out rather uncertainly.

'Nothing my dear Miss Frayle,' observed the Doctor, 'could be more uncharacteristic of you.'

Miss Frayle still looked doubtful, as if she were not quite sure of what would be the reception accorded to the suggestion which she was about to make.

'Well,' she said hesitatingly, 'would you really like to have me back with you in my old position permanently?'

It is possible that Doctor Morelle was about to utter something extremely unusual — a compliment, no less. He had in fact begun by saying: 'My dear Miss Frayle, nothing would give me more — ' when the telephone rang.

'Confound the thing!' he snapped, and then added: 'Would you be so kind as to answer it, Miss Frayle?'

Miss Frayle lifted the receiver. 'Hello?' she said brightly. 'Yes, this is Doctor Morelle's house. Who is that, please?'

The news was obviously not good, as a look of surprised alarm came over her face. 'Good heavens!' she exclaimed. 'Yes, yes, I'll tell the Doctor at once. Hold on, please.'

She turned to him with anxious eyes. 'It's some young woman, Doctor,' she explained. 'She says that Professor Raymond has been found shot. She says that he is a patient of yours and that you know him well.'

Even Doctor Morelle seemed to be shaken out of his customary indifference.

'Raymond, the zoological man?'

Miss Frayle nodded silently.

'Shot?' he repeated.

He grasped the receiver with a firm hand, and listened to the somewhat frightened voice from the other end. 'Doctor Morelle here now,' he said. 'I see. Very well. I understand. I'll come along without delay.'

'What's happened, Doctor?' Miss Frayle asked anxiously, as he replaced the receiver.

'No time to waste with questions, Miss Frayle,' he snapped. 'My case, hat, coat, and a taxi. Quickly.' Then he suddenly remembered. 'That is,' he added, in considerably more polite tones, 'if you would be so kind as to assist, Miss Frayle.'

Miss Frayle laughed. 'All right, Doctor,' she said. 'I'll do my best. And where does this Professor Raymond live?'

'In Hampstead,' Doctor Morelle said. 'In one of those streets overlooking the Heath.'

'Wouldn't it be quicker, Doctor,' Miss Frayle suggested, 'if you would whistle up the taxi while I am getting your things together for you?'

'Whistle up a taxi?' the Doctor repeated

in amazed tones. 'I? Oh, very well, Miss Frayle. I'll see what I can do in that way.'

Actually, Doctor Morelle proved highly successful, and managed to secure a taxi in a matter of two minutes — no mean feat in Harley Street in the middle of the afternoon.

In a few minutes they drew up in a pleasant little street in Hampstead.

'This right, sir?' queried the driver.

'Almost right,' the Doctor conceded. 'If you will kindly drive about two hundred yards farther down the street, we should be at the residence which we are seeking.'

The taxi-man drove the distance indicated, and then stopped again.

'Okay now, sir?'

'Indubitably,' agreed Doctor Morelle. He paid the driver and then led the way towards the house, turning away inside the gate and making for the side of the house.

'What a lovely rambling old house, Doctor Morelle,' Miss Frayle remarked, gazing at it almost goggle-eyed with admiration. 'And right overlooking the Heath, too. How absolutely delightful it must be to live here!'

Then she realised the direction in which the Doctor was leading her and added: 'But why are you going this way, Doctor? Isn't that the front door, over there?'

'It is sometimes instructive,' Doctor Morelle explained patiently, 'to effect one's entrance from a not altogether expected quarter. These French windows, which I happen to know lead to the Professor's library, are open, and present an ideal opportunity of making an unexpected entry into Professor Raymond's residence. Follow me.'

He marched off in the direction indicated, with Miss Frayle obediently trotting at his heels. Suddenly a curious noise smote their ears.

Miss Frayle started. 'Oooh!' she squealed. 'What on earth was that noise?'

'Merely a horse,' Doctor Morelle said in tones that were meant to be soothing but which proved to suggest extreme irritation. 'Those buildings over there, at the extreme end of the house are the stables.'

The shrill neigh of the horse was repeated, and, in spite of the fact that she was now in possession of a full explanation of the noise Miss Frayle found herself shuddering again.

'It has such a very high note. Doctor,' she said in nervous tones.

'No doubt,' retorted the Doctor with what might have been termed a grin, 'because it is a somewhat tall horse!'

Miss Frayle had no answer to this but a giggle. It was the first time for a long time that she had heard Doctor Morelle make a joke. But, contrary to the popular belief, Doctor Morelle has a sense of humour, though it is a moderately mordant one.

However, he did not permit his sense of humour to divert him from the pursuit of any task that he had set himself.

'Let us enter the library,' he said, making his way to the open French windows, and stepping into the room, Miss Frayle still close upon his heels.

'Oh! Who are you?' said a startled voice.

Doctor Morelle looked at the young man who had been not unnaturally surprised at their entry in such a completely unorthodox manner.

'I am Doctor Morelle. This is Miss Frayle, my secretary.'

'Oh, of course, Doctor,' the young man said, with infinite relief in his tones and with a more settled expression on his bronzed, clean-shaven face. 'I was, of course, expecting you, but I didn't anticipate you would come in that way.'

Miss Frayle apparently considered it was up to her to offer some sort of apology on behalf of the Doctor's infringement of the ordinary rules of courteous behaviour.

'The front door was shut, you see,' she explained in nervous tones. 'We didn't want to trouble anyone, you'll understand, so we thought that we — '

Doctor Morelle ruthlessly cut in on this rambling explanation.

'Miss Frayle,' he said, 'is apologising for my perhaps unusual mode of ingress. Such an apology is, of course, totally unnecessary since I have already explained to you that *I* am Doctor Morelle!'

'Oh,' said the young man, still,

apparently, not finding the identity of the great man quite sufficient explanation of his unorthodox conduct.

'Well, really!' Miss Frayle murmured, as if she found the Doctor's egotism at this point well-nigh insufferable.

'You were saying, Miss Frayle?' the Doctor remarked suavely. His sharp ear rarely missed anything.

'Nothing, nothing!' she exclaimed hurriedly.

The young man was saying:

'I'm Geoffrey Curtis. I am Professor Raymond's nephew. You may possibly have heard him speak of me from time to time, Doctor.'

'I think that I can recall such occasions to mind,' Doctor Morelle said non-committally.

'The Professor is still unconscious, I'm afraid,' Curtis explained. 'I think you had better come up to the bedroom straight away. Perhaps Miss Frayle would prefer to stay down here while you perform your examination, Doctor?'

Doctor Morelle had no intention of allowing anything of the sort to happen.

'I may require Miss Frayle's assistance, Mr. Curtis,' he said. 'She is not entirely unused to accompanying me on occasions of this character.'

'I shan't faint at the first sight of blood, if that's what you mean, Mr. Curtis,' said Miss Frayle with a smile. 'That is probably what was worrying you. I may be Frayle by name, you know, but I'm not necessarily frail by nature!'

'Well, really!' murmured Doctor Morelle, who had been known to observe that the pun is the lowest form of humour.

'Did you say something, Doctor?' Miss Frayle inquired Her ears were not so acute as the Doctor's.

'Nothing, nothing!' he exclaimed hurriedly.

'Perhaps you'll come this way, then,' Geoffrey Curtis said leading the way to the door.

He went up the stairs, where Miss Frayle observed the thick crimson carpet and the pleasant water colours which lined the walls at intervals. Obviously, she told herself, a place owned by a man of real taste.

On the landing the Professor's nephew

led the way to a door at the end of a short corridor.

'In here, Doctor.'

Doctor Morelle looked down at the prostrate figure on the bed. His old friend was unconscious, though not it seemed injured in any serious way.

'My wife and I fixed the bandage the best we could,' Curtis explained. 'Not very expert, I'm afraid.'

'Adequate enough for its immediate purpose, I assure you,' Doctor Morelle remarked in conversational tones. He then proceeded to examine the wound. 'Shoulder somewhat badly lacerated I see,' he added to himself. 'Only a flesh wound, however. Some considerable loss of blood, though the shot did not penetrate very deeply.' He turned to Miss Frayle. 'Is that the Professor's jacket on that chair?' he asked. 'Miss Frayle, I wonder if you would be so kind as to hand it over to me?'

But Miss Frayle was apparently in no condition to hand over anything. She was swaying on her feet and her face had gone deathly white.

'She's fainting!' exclaimed Curtis.

'How extremely irritating!' the Doctor said. 'Sit down Miss Frayle, and put your head between your knees quickly. Then you will soon recover.'

Miss Frayle obeyed orders, sitting on a chair, and putting her head in the position indicated.

'Shall I get you some water?' asked Curtis somewhat anxiously, looking at her white face.

'No, thank you,' Miss Frayle said. 'I shall be all right in a minute.'

Doctor Morelle had found this interruption somewhat irritating.

'Yes, yes. Leave her alone. She will recover her equilibrium in a comparatively short time,' he said. 'Hand me the Professor's coat, would you, Mr. Curtis?'

'Here it is, Doctor.'

Doctor Morelle examined the coat with some care, while Curtis continued to stare anxiously at Miss Frayle.

'Are you sure you're all right, Miss Frayle?' he asked quietly, while Doctor Morelle was looking at the jacket with the most minute attention.

'I'm much better already,' Miss Frayle reassured him.

Doctor Morelle continued to examine the coat.

'Considerable scorching, indicating that the gun was discharged at very close quarters,' he announced at length, holding up the jacket so that Curtis could see the burn that he had been so carefully studying. The Professor's nephew nodded.

'The nature of the wound,' the Doctor went on, 'would seen to indicate that the firearm used to produce it was almost certainly a shotgun.'

'You think the Professor will be all right?' Curtis asked in anxious tones.

'I can certainly assure you of that,' the Doctor said. 'He is suffering from severe shock, which is, of course, quite understandable. But if he has complete rest and quiet, he should be perfectly all right in a matter of a few days from now. But how, precisely, did the incident leading to such a regrettable result occur?'

'I'm afraid I can't tell you very much about that,' admitted Curtis. 'I heard the shot when I was in the library. It sounded to me as if it came from the direction of the greenhouse just outside. I rushed around and found my uncle unconscious on the floor of the greenhouse.'

'And the firearm?' queried Doctor Morelle.

'A double-barrelled shotgun was lying on the floor beside him.'

'It had been discharged?'

'Yes. One barrel only.'

Miss Frayle looked at him in an understanding way, as if the explanation of these tragic events had suddenly occurred to her mind.

'You mean that he had been cleaning it, and it had gone off accidentally?' she said.

'Ah!' snapped the Doctor. 'Miss Frayle is now herself again. That is splendid!'

'That,' Curtis said slowly, 'is what I find so very difficult to understand. You see, Uncle was always so careful handling guns. It seems to me to be almost impossible that such an accident could possibly have happened to him.'

Doctor Morelle, for the first time since he had examined the Professor's coat, looked interested.

'What possible alternative explanation had you in mind, Mr. Curtis?' he asked.

'Well,' answered Curtis in hesitating tones. 'I wondered after all, whether the true explanation might not be that someone might have deliberately shot him.'

'Good heavens!' exclaimed Miss Frayle, as if she thought such an explanation far too horrible to be believed.

'I trust that you are not feeling faint again, my dear Miss Frayle?' said Doctor Morelle. Miss Frayle was not quite sure whether this was pure solicitude on her behalf or whether the Doctor was being his normal sarcastic self.

'Of course not!' she retorted.

Doctor Morelle accordingly proceeded to ignore her and went on to ask further questions from the Professor's nephew.

'Do you suspect any particular person of being the assailant of the Professor?' he asked.

Curtis thought for a few moments before replying. There was a definite trace of uncertainty (which did not escape the Doctor's attention) in the young man's voice when he managed to formulate his reply.

'No,' he said, and paused. 'No one that I can think of,' he added.

'How many members of the household are there?' asked Doctor Morelle. It was clear he thought there were some important facts that he had as yet not ascertained.

'There are my wife and myself,' Curtis replied. 'We've been staying here for the last couple of weeks, you know. Then there is the housekeeper. And there is a daily help, but she only comes in for the mornings.'

Miss Frayle refused to be kept out of the conversation indefinitely.

'Who was it that telephoned about the Professor?' she asked. 'The voice sounded to me like that of quite a young woman.'

'Oh, that was my wife,' Curtis explained. 'I'm afraid she has been rather upset by what happened, and after we had managed to get Uncle up here on the bed I thought she had better lie down for a bit.'

Miss Frayle murmured something, she was always sympathetic with any fellow-creature in distress.

'She had a splitting headache, and no wonder, for it was a nasty shock for us all. But, in spite of her headache, she insisted on 'phoning you first.'

Doctor Morelle apparently thought this diversion had been going on long enough. It was high time, in his opinion, that they got back to the main line of investigation.

'What about outside staff?' he asked.

'There's a gardener, an old boy, who has worked for the Professor for years,' Curtis said. 'And a younger fellow — he's new. Gives a hand in the garden and helps in the stables, and does odd jobs generally.' Curtis stopped and slapped his hand on his knee. 'Come to think of it,' he said, 'that young chap must have seen the Professor just before the — er — accident took place,'

There was no doubt about the extreme interest of Doctor Morelle to this revelation. His normally expressionless face lit up.

'Explain,' he said.

'Well,' Curtis replied, 'Uncle asked me to find North — that's the young chap's name — about half an hour before he was shot. Apparently he wanted to talk to him about the arrival of the giraffes.'

'Giraffes?' queried Miss Frayle in surprise.

'Yes, two young giraffes which have just arrived from Africa,' Curtis said with a smile. 'They were some sort of present, given to Uncle by some learned society out there, as a recognition of the work he has done for zoology. You know the sort of thing that is sometimes done. Uncle won't be able to keep them, of course, He's arranging for them to go to the Zoo; they'll be moved over in the matter of a day or two. Meanwhile, they have been out in the big barn behind the stables.'

Miss Frayle clapped her hands together with delight. 'Two giraffes!' she exclaimed. 'Oh, I would love to see them!' Then another idea suddenly came to her. 'Doctor!' she said in excited tones. 'That was what we heard just as we arrived. And you said that it was a horse neighing!'

'A *tall* horse, Miss Frayle,' the Doctor reminded her.

'Now, you're trying to wangle out of it!' Miss Frayle said. 'A horse! Dear, dear — !'

Doctor Morelle interposed another remark at this point.

'Possibly a brief interview with the young gardener you have been discussing would prove helpful in the present circumstances.'

'You think so?'

'I should have thought that the conclusion was abundantly obvious,' the Doctor said.

'I'll get him for you,' Curtis said. 'I imagine that you would prefer to interview him in the library.'

'It would appear to be the most suitable room for the purpose,' Doctor Morelle said. 'And while I am conducting the interview — and if you would manage to condescend to give the matter your full attention, my dear Miss Frayle — I think that it would be advisable to telephone for a nurse.'

'Of course, Doctor,' Miss Frayle agreed hurriedly. She was compelled to admit to herself in all candour that her attention had been wandering somewhat from the matter in hand. And it was typical of Doctor Morelle that, in spite of his concentration on the shooting, Miss Frayle's wandering mind had not escaped his attention.

'I want the nurse to be on duty in this room by the time the patient recovers consciousness,' the Doctor explained.

'And now,' Curtis went on, 'if you'll follow me to the library I will arrange for the gardener to be sent to you.'

Miss Frayle had thought that Doctor Morelle's study was the most book-filled room in London; but Professor Raymond's study appeared almost more so. The whole of the space on the walls, from floor to ceiling, was filled with books, for the most part leather-bound volumes of the proceedings of the learned societies whose subjects were the lifework of Professor Raymond.

Here, in a few minutes, came North — a young countryman clearly somewhat out of place in London. He stood awkwardly, and kept moving uneasily from one foot to the other.

'You have not been here long, I understand?' Doctor Morelle began by asking.

'Been here only a week, Doctor,' he said. 'Before that I was working down in Surrey, just outside Dorking. My name's North, Arthur North, and I'm twenty-six years old — '

Doctor Morelle interrupted him. 'I don't think that anything in the nature of a full-length autobiography is really necessary,' he said. 'Mr. Curtis informed me that you probably saw your employer, Professor Raymond, immediately before the unfortunate accident took place.'

'Will he die?'

'I would remind you that I am asking the questions,' snapped the Doctor.

'I only wanted to know,' North explained in a voice that had almost become a whine. 'Always very decent to me the Professor was, and I shouldn't like to think that he — '

Doctor Morelle interrupted him again. 'You will no doubt recall that he sent for you in connection with the two giraffes which have recently arrived here from Africa. He interviewed you, I understand, in the greenhouse. Am I correct in my assumptions?'

'That's right,' said North. 'He wanted to know how I was managing with the two giraffes, and if they were okay in the barn where they'd been put.'

'I see,' Doctor Morelle commented. 'That is eminently satisfactory. You were able to reassure him as to the condition of the giraffes?'

'That's right,' North said again. 'They're queer animals, and I never dealt with such things before. Anyhow, it didn't matter much, because they're being moved to the Zoo in a matter of two or three days. Don't suppose they'd pine away and die in that time.'

'Did you notice,' went on the Doctor, 'if your employer was occupying himself in cleaning any firearms while he was talking to you about these giraffes?'

'That's right,' North agreed readily enough. 'That's what he was doing.'

'And what particular firearm was engaging his attention when you were with him?'

'A double-barrelled shotgun.'

'This one?' Doctor Morelle asked, producing the gun.

'I didn't look at it specially,' North said. 'But it was just like that. I daresay that was the one, because I don't suppose that there's more than one in the house anyhow.'

Doctor Morelle pondered this for a moment before resuming the cross-examination.

Then he said: 'And after you had finished this conversation about the two giraffes you returned to your work?'

'That's right,' said North. It seemed to be his standard reply to all the questions that might be addressed to him.

'You saw no one on your way?'

'No. I just went straight to the barn.'

Again Doctor Morelle seemed to find considerable food for thought in these replies, for he was silent for some considerable time after the last remark from North.

Then he went on: 'According to Mr. Curtis, until he intimated to you a few minutes ago that I required to see you, you were ignorant of the fact that Professor Raymond had been a victim of an accident with a shotgun.'

'That's right,' North said once more. 'Fair knocked me down with a feather, you could have, when I heard that the old boy had been shot.'

'Everyone else in the vicinity of the house,' Doctor Morelle pointed out, with more than his usual patience, 'heard the report of the firearm. I should not have thought you have any trace of deafness.'

'I told you,' said North, 'I was in the barn. That's a hundred yards or more from the greenhouse.'

'True,' the Doctor agreed. 'But not out of hearing of the report of the gun, I should surmise.'

'Well, there was them giraffes, you know,' North said. 'Fair squawking their heads off, they was. I suppose that they got hungry and wanted their food. They fair yelped the place down. So I never heard nothing what was going on outside the barn just then.'

Much to Doctor Morelle's annoyance — for he thought that the conversation was just reaching the point where it might yield interesting results — the door opened suddenly. The Doctor did not exhibit the annoyance that he felt at the interruption. The newcomer was Curtis.

'Uncle seems to be on the point of regaining consciousness, Doctor,' he said excitedly. 'Don't you think that you had better come up to the bedroom at once?'

North said: 'So he ain't going to die, Mr. Curtis?'

Doctor Morelle looked his inimitable sardonic self as he added: 'Which is somewhat unfortunate for a certain person.'

'What do you mean?' North gasped.

'I merely mean that Professor Raymond, when he regains consciousness, will be able to identify his assailant.'

'Then someone did shoot him?' Curtis exclaimed, in surprised tones.

North had crossed the room and suddenly he grabbed the shotgun, one barrel of which had not been fired, and pointed it at Curtis.

'As if you didn't know!' he exclaimed. 'Come on, Mr. Curtis, put your hands up — and quick!'

'Are you mad? Put that gun down, North, before there's more trouble.'

Curtis had gone deathly pale.

'Do as I say!' North growled. 'If you don't you'll get the same as you give the poor old Professor. Okay, Doctor, you can get on with the 'phoning for the cops. I'll keep him covered while you do it.'

'You blasted fool, North, are you going to put that gun down right away?' Curtis blustered.

'That I'm not!' North said grimly. 'You may have tried to kill the Professor, but I'm damned if you're going to have the chance to try to kill me.'

Again the door opened, this time to admit Miss Frayle. 'The nurse is on her way round now, Doctor,' she began, and then suddenly realised the dramatic scene that she was interrupting. 'Good gracious' she exclaimed in alarm. 'What on earth is happening, Doctor Morelle?'

'It's all right, Miss,' North said gruffly. 'You won't come to any harm. I've got him covered.'

'It would appear, my dear Miss Frayle,' Doctor Morelle remarked with his normal suavity, 'that we have succeeded in trapping the person responsible for the

111

shooting of Professor Raymond, and that it would be as well if you would perform your customary task of getting Scotland Yard on the telephone without undue delay.'

*   *   *

It was a short while afterwards when Inspector Hood entered the room.

'Got a criminal for us again, Doctor?' he said.

The Doctor nodded. 'Professor Raymond has been shot, fortunately without fatal results. But I think that a charge of attempted murder is what is indicated at the moment.'

'That's right,' said North. 'I've got him covered.'

'I hope you're right,' the man from Scotland Yard said. He had known Doctor Morelle for many years and, while he had a great respect for the Doctor's intellectual powers, he was always afraid that sooner or later he would be driven into making an arrest on grounds not strictly justifiable from the legal point of view.

'And the charge is attempted murder?' the Inspector said. He was making his way to Curtis's side, when the Doctor suddenly interrupted him.

'You're arresting the wrong man, Inspector,' he said. 'Arthur North is the criminal.'

Miss Frayle saw North, who had been holding the gun so firmly, sag at the knees. His body lost its rigidity, and he collapsed in a chair as the Inspector crossed to him.

After he had been taken away, Miss Frayle turned towards her employer.

'What a fool he was,' she said, 'to think that he could pull the wool over your eyes, Doctor.'

'Too many people, my dear Miss Frayle, are all too easily deceived by my unassuming and modest manner.'

Miss Frayle was unable entirely to suppress the giggle that rose unbidden to her lips. 'You?' she said; 'Unassuming! Unobtrusive! I mean — er — that is — ' She broke off.

'Pray proceed, my dear Miss Frayle. No doubt you were about to say that you knew North had been discovered by Professor Raymond to be a thief, that he was to be dismissed without notice and without references, and that he merely tried to brazen it out by accusing Mr. Curtis, here, of the crime.'

For once Miss Frayle was speechless, and Doctor Morelle went on, 'I seem to recall, Miss Frayle, that even you were convinced I was unable to distinguish between a horse's neigh and a giraffe's squawk — as North described it. What a completely ludicrous attempt at an alibi! North told me he failed to hear the report of the gun when he was in the barn because the giraffes made so much noise yelping their heads off.' It was not often that Doctor Morelle laughed aloud, but now he did so. It was a matter of a minute or two before Miss Frayle was able to say another word.

'But what is so funny about that, Doctor?' she asked, when at length his laughter had subsided to a chuckle.

'Merely, my dear Miss Frayle,' the Doctor purred, 'that long-necked African ungulates happen to be almost entirely mute. The only sound which they are able to utter being a very faint mew which would quite certainly not drown the report of a shotgun.'

'Giraffes dumb!' Miss Frayle remarked. 'Just fancy! I never knew that.'

Once again the Doctor laughed loud and long.

Miss Frayle looked somewhat thoughtful. 'Come to think of it' she muttered, 'being secretary to a long-necked African thingumebob would make rather a nice change.'

5

The Hanging Guardian

Miss Frayle was never able to be quite sure whether Doctor Morelle truly appreciated what she did for him. His naturally sarcastic tongue was an efficient method of hiding his feelings.

She came into his study slowly, notebook and pencil in one hand, while the other hand nervously adjusted the spectacles on her nose — a habit of hers which the Doctor invariably found a source of extreme irritation.

'Well, well, well,' she said, as she settled herself in the chair opposite him. 'The first day back at my old job.'

The Doctor gave her a non-committal glance.

'It's quite a moment. Don't you agree, Doctor Morelle?' She was unable to resist studying his face as she made this remark.

'It is indeed a gratifying occasion, Miss

Frayle,' Doctor Morelle replied with at any rate an approach to cordiality. 'It is an occasion, I may say, to which I have been looking forward with some considerable feeling of pleasurable anticipation.'

'Have you really, Doctor?' Miss Frayle was thrilled, not to say surprised. This was quite the nearest approach to a pretty speech Doctor Morelle had ever made to her during their long association.

'I know,' he said solemnly, 'that I should never have found anyone as suitable for the position of my secretary as yourself.'

'Somehow,' said Miss Frayle, with what seemed, for a moment, to be an echo of his own sarcastic tone, 'I'd rather gathered that.'

Doctor Morelle coughed and looked at her with what in an ordinary individual would have been termed surprise.

'By the way,' Miss Frayle went on, 'I do hope, if I may say so, you won't be having quite so many of these dreadfully bloodthirsty crimes to deal with.'

'And why do you express that hope, pray?'

'I mean to say, it did get a trifle nerve-racking sometimes.'

The Doctor looked at her with a grim smile. 'My dear Miss Frayle,' he said in rasping tones, 'some men are born detectives, some achieve detective genius, and some have it thrust upon them.'

'Sounds almost like a quotation from Shakespeare, you know, Doctor,' Miss Frayle remarked in her most innocent manner.

'The cases which I have investigated in recent years,' the Doctor went on, 'have been invariably successful, even though their investigation has never been of my seeking.'

'Yes, yes, I know, Doctor. You just attract murder and all the other horrors like a magnet.'

Doctor Morelle eyed her with a slight air of disapproval.

'That observation, Miss Frayle, if I may say so, has a somewhat ambiguous ring.'

At that moment the telephone rang.

Miss Frayle said with a gentle smile: 'Anyway, I hope that there is nothing ambiguous — or whatever was the word that you used — about this 'phone ring!

'Hello? This is Doctor Morelle's house. What? Hold on, please.'

She turned to Doctor Morelle, holding her hand over the receiver. 'It's the Regal Hotel, Doctor,' she explained. 'It is the manager speaking. He said that he wants to have a word with you at once.'

The Doctor took the receiver from her with an irritable gesture.

'Doctor Morelle here. Yes, yes. I understand. I will be there without delay.' He slammed the receiver down.

Miss Frayle's eyes opened wide. 'Is anything wrong' she asked.

'Why, otherwise, do you imagine they would be telephoning so urgently for a doctor?'

'I do hope it is nothing — er — nothing — nothing which one could call nasty.'

'That, my dear Miss Frayle, would depend upon your definition of that word. There is nothing which I, at any rate, would term nasty.'

'That makes a change, anyway!' Miss Frayle exclaimed

'One of the guests at the hotel has

apparently been trying a little experiment,' he continued.

'An experiment?' Miss Frayle asked innocently.

'The experiment entailed the using of a rope instead of a necktie!'

'You mean that he has hanged himself!'

'An extremely brilliant deduction, my dear Miss Frayle,' the Doctor complimented her with heavy sarcasm. 'Really, I feel that you are in the course of becoming quite an efficient detective yourself.'

'That's what I'm afraid of,' Miss Frayle complained. 'I don't in the least want to be a detective, Doctor. I just want to be a quiet, ordinary efficient secretary, left to get on with my work in peace.'

The remark stung Doctor Morelle into a retort of even more than his usual acidity.

'In that case,' he snarled, 'why have you been so constantly badgering me in this last few weeks to allow you to return to your former position here?'

Miss Frayle goggled at him indignantly. 'Well, I like that!' she exclaimed. '*I've* been badgering *you*! When you have been nagging at me all the time to come back here!'

Doctor Morelle's expression became frosty. 'This,' he said. 'is turning into an argument as acrimonious as it is unseemly, Miss Frayle. I fear it will never be established with any accuracy which of us initiated your return to your post here. I think the question might well be omitted from all future discussions. Let us obtain a taxi and investigate this little matter at the Regal Hotel.'

Arrived at the hotel, Doctor Morelle made his way to the inquiry desk, and asked to be taken at once to the manager's office. This proved to be on the ground floor, just off the impressive-looking foyer in which they were standing.

The Doctor and Miss Frayle were received by a very worried looking man. He was dressed impeccably and in normal circumstances he would have been, Miss Frayle decided, quite handsome. But his face was now clouded with anxiety.

'I think,' Doctor Morelle said, 'it would

be as well if you would endeavour to give me a complete account of everything that has happened in connection with this unfortunate affair. Give me the facts, even though it may possibly appear to you that they are not germane to the immediate issue.'

'It was about two hours ago when Mr. Harrison was discovered by the waitress. She went in as usual with his breakfast, and found him hanging from his wardrobe. She was very upset, of course.'

'I should think she would be!' Miss Frayle declared feelingly.

Doctor Morelle snapped: 'We can safely dispense with the description of the young woman's not altogether unnatural hysterics. And also I think that it would be as well to adjourn to the room in question, since there it is more simple to get the matter into its correct perspective.'

'This way,' said the manager, and led them to a pleasant room sunny and cheerful, and opulently furnished.

'This is the wardrobe from which Mr. Harrison was hanging I presume?' the

Doctor asked, glancing round the room.

'Yes.'

Doctor Morelle examined the wardrobe with some care, though Miss Frayle was unable to imagine just what he hoped to see that would help him to solve the mystery.

'You called in a doctor, and the police?' he was saying.

'Yes, of course, we have a resident doctor here — this is a very large hotel.'

Doctor Morelle snorted with impatience. 'Considering that the hotel more or less dominates Oxford Street, its size had not altogether eluded me!'

Miss Frayle murmured soothingly: 'I'm sure, Doctor, that the manager is only trying to tell you exactly what happened as you asked him to do.'

'I am merely trying to ascertain why, since there was a doctor already on the spot, it had been deemed necessary that I also should be called into the case.'

'I should, perhaps, explain,' the other said hastily, 'that I am in actual fact only the assistant manager here, the manager himself is away ill, and I am afraid I felt the responsibility of this awful business. So I thought it would be a good plan if you were to represent the hotel at the inquest.'

'Rather a good idea,' Miss Frayle commented.

Doctor Morelle did not seem altogether to share Miss Frayle's enthusiasm for the role that had been proposed for him, although he made no comment.

'The body has been removed, of course,' he said. 'And I may, I take it, presume that the police have now concluded their examination?'

The other nodded. 'They went only a few minutes before your arrival, Doctor.'

'How long had the deceased been staying here?' the Doctor asked.

'About a year. And for the whole time he has occupied this particular suite.'

Miss Frayle asked:

'Are there any relatives, or anyone else who is interested in the poor man?'

'I believe he had a brother and a sister who paid him a visit occasionally, though they did not come here with any sort of regularity.'

'I presume that Mr. Harrison would be a man of some means,' went on Doctor Morelle. 'Had he entrusted any valuables or documents of any kind to your care, for locking in the hotel safe?'

'We've nothing of his in the safe, I remember the manager saying to me some time ago that Mr. Harrison kept some jewellery of some kind in his bedroom. But I'm afraid that I don't know any details. Why are you interested in that point? You're not suggesting his death was anything but suicide, are you, Doctor?'

Doctor Morelle snapped: 'I am not in the habit of offering conjectures on such matters.'

He added: 'You referred a few moments ago to the deceased's relatives having paid him occasional, though irregular, visits. Might I enquire whether anyone called on him this morning?'

'Not so far as I am aware.'

'Still,' commented Miss Frayle, with her air of stating the obvious as if it were some astonishingly original discovery, 'in a place as large as this it would be easy for anyone knowing the number of the room just to walk upstairs and come straight in without being seen or suspected at all.'

'I suppose they could,' the assistant manager said slowly.

'Were you yourself well acquainted with Mr. Harrison?' was Doctor Morelle's next question.

'No. In fact, I don't think I'd ever met him. The manager knew him well, however. I believe that he was quite a friend of his.'

While Doctor Morelle was pondering this reply the door opened suddenly.

A young man bustled in excitedly. His hair was untidy and his tie was under his ear.

'I want to see Mr. Harrison — and to see him quickly!'

'May I ask you why, sir?' the assistant manager said.

'He's my guardian.'

'Your guardian?' Doctor Morelle studied the newcomer with considerable interest. Rather, Miss Frayle thought, as he would have studied a strange specimen under the microscope.

'My name's Carter. I happened to buy the midday edition of one of the evening papers, just as I was passing, and I read all about his death.'

'How awful for you!' exclaimed Miss Frayle sympathetically.

'Most horrible shock it was,' Carter agreed. 'I came up right away. Until I saw it in the Stop Press, as a matter of fact I'd not even got an idea of where he was living. I've been away from England for some years. South America. The last I heard from him or of him, was about two years back. It's all the more terrible for me really, since I only arrived in England this morning. Got into Tilbury in the small hours, and came straight up to London. And then — this.'

'This is a most unfortunate affair for you, Mr. — ' The assistant manager paused.

'Carter. Edward Carter.'

'Mr. Carter. As you already know, your guardian is dead and the body has been taken away for a post-mortem examination.'

'It's almost impossible to believe it's

happened,' Carter exclaimed. 'I was so much looking forward to seeing him again.'

'You say the last occasion upon which you communicated with Mr. Harrison was two years ago?' the Doctor asked.

'No, Doctor Morelle,' corrected Miss Frayle. 'He said that was the last time he'd heard from him or of him.'

'Thank you, Miss Frayle!'

'That's just it!' exclaimed Carter. 'I wrote to him several times afterwards, but for some reason he never replied to me.'

'May I enquire the reason for Mr. Harrison's silence?' Doctor Morelle asked.

Carter paused before he said, slowly and somewhat reluctantly: 'I offended him — quite without meaning to do so — and I suppose he just wouldn't accept the explanations I wrote him. It's really grim to think of him dying, all alone like this, without having done something to patch up our silly quarrel which, in any case, was all over nothing.' He went on, with a deep sigh: 'I suppose there's nothing that I can do about it now. I — I think I'd like to have a drink, I feel just about all in. If you don't mind I'll go down to the bar. I'll be back with you again in a few minutes.'

He looked pale and haggard, as if the shock of his guardian's death had proved temporarily too much for him. He moved slowly to the door. Miss Frayle looked after him with eyes wide with sympathy behind her horn-rims.

After the door had closed on him she sighed.

'What a dreadful thing,' she said, 'to come all the way from South America, and then to find his guardian — '

The door opened again and a tall, handsome woman came slowly into the room.

'I beg your pardon,' she said quietly. 'But — '

'Oh, good gracious!' Miss Frayle was exclaiming, startled by this new arrival.

'I'm sorry if I startled you,' the woman said.

'Are you looking for someone, Madam?' the assistant manager asked.

'Mr. Harrison, please.'

'You know him?' Doctor Morelle snapped.

'I'm his sister.' She paused and looked round at them. 'Where is my brother? He was expecting me to call and see him today.'

Miss Frayle said: 'I'm afraid he's — he's — he was found this morning, Miss Harrison.'

'I don't understand what you mean. Do you mean that he is dead?'

'This will be a fearful shock for you, I'm afraid,' Miss Frayle went on quietly. 'But it appears as if he had taken his own life.'

'My brother — suicide? That is absolutely impossible for me to believe.'

'Nevertheless, I fear that it is true,' Doctor Morelle said.

'But why?' demanded the other, her voice rising. 'Why? Why should he commit suicide? When I last saw him — only about ten days ago — he was well and happy. Why should his outlook change so suddenly, in a matter of a few days?'

'You ask why he should have committed suicide, Madam,' the Doctor said. 'That is a question which I fear I am unable to answer at the moment. I had, indeed, hoped that you yourself might be able to offer some information which would assist us in getting some explanation of what otherwise seems totally inexplicable.'

'Arthur killing himself!' the woman was muttering half to herself. 'No, no! I just can't make myself believe it.'

The door opened again, and Carter came in.

'I say!' he remarked. 'I'm afraid that I must have taken the wrong turning. I seem to have been walking around in circles since I left you just now!' And then, turning round, gazed in surprise at the woman,

'Edward!' she gasped.

'You!' he exclaimed.

'You would turn up out of the blue now of all times!' the other said bitterly. 'After giving him, and all of us, so much cause to suffer!'

'Surely,' Carter said quietly and soothingly, 'this is not the occasion for raking up old grievances of this kind. I'm absolutely broken up by the news.'

But she was not to be placated. 'I'd like to know,' she said, 'how long you've been hanging about waiting for him to die.'

'You won't do any good talking like that,' Carter retorted. 'If you want to know, I only arrived in England this morning, landed at Tilbury, and came straight on up to London. I was coming to see — '

She cut him short. 'He'd have kicked you out, and you know it, Edward! He never wanted anything more to do with you!'

The assistant manager was finding this scene increasingly embarrassing. 'Miss Harrison, Mr. Carter,' he expostulated. 'Please! Surely this is not the time and the place to indulge in recriminations of this kind.'

Without staying to listen to anything more, Doctor Morelle silently grasped Miss Frayle's arm and led her towards the door. The others were so involved in their argument that they did not notice what the Doctor and Miss Frayle were doing.

As he closed the door behind him, Doctor Morelle murmured: 'Miss Frayle.'

'Yes, Doctor?'

'I think that I observed a telephone in the sitting room.'

Miss Frayle looked more than a little surprised. 'But why do you want a telephone now, Doctor?' she asked.

'While they are engaged in that regrettable altercation,' he explained, 'it would appear to be an appropriate opportunity to telephone the police.'

'But the police already have the matter in hand,' Miss Frayle objected.

'Have they?'

'Yes. The assistant manager told us, don't you remember? They left only just before we arrived here.'

'Nevertheless, would you, without any delay, get in touch with Scotland Yard, Miss Frayle?'

'But whatever for?'

Doctor Morelle snapped: 'If you hasten, Scotland Yard should arrive before the person I suspect of being implicated in the murder takes leave of the hotel.'

'Murder!' Miss Frayle's eyes were saucer-like. 'Oh, well,' she said, giving in, 'I suppose you're right as usual.'

And she dialled the number.

'Pending the arrival of the gentlemen from Scotland Yard,' he said, 'I would suggest that you go to the street and endeavour with your usual efficiency to procure a taxi for our homeward journey. When I have given the police the necessary information, I will join you in the vehicle which by that time should be awaiting me.'

'But — but — I should like to know how you decided it was murder.'

'All in good time, Miss Frayle. First of all, if you would be so kind, the taxi!'

* * *

It was only about ten minutes before he joined her in the taxi she had procured. He wore a smirk of satisfaction on his face — an expression with which, in the course of time, Miss Frayle had become painfully familiar.

'Now, Doctor,' she said, 'can you tell me how you decided it was murder?'

'The guilty person was palpably Edward Carter, the deceased man's ward.'

'It wasn't at all palpable to me, I'm afraid,' Miss Frayle said.

'I'd made up my mind, as soon as you gave the impression that you thought it was a murder, that the manager was the person who had done it.'

Doctor Morelle smiled sarcastically. That smile Miss Frayle now knew to be the inevitable prelude to a remark that would be especially crushing.

'I feel sure, my dear Miss Frayle,' he said, 'that one of these days you may yet catch yourself unawares, and so spot the criminal correctly.'

Miss Frayle was not quite sure whether this was pure sarcasm, or whether the remark was in the nature of a compliment.

'That'll be the day, won't it, Doctor?'

'When he was arrested,' the Doctor went on, 'Carter made a complete confession of his guilt.'

'Did he?'

'He confessed that he had in fact never lost track of his guardian's whereabouts. He had, as he told us, arrived in London only this morning. His first action on arrival was to go to the hotel and make his way unseen (in the manner so sapiently suggested by yourself, Miss Frayle) up to his guardian's room.'

Miss Frayle preened herself slightly. This was, indeed, something not unlike a genuine compliment!

'And what happened then?' she asked.

Doctor Morelle resumed his exposition. 'A bitter quarrel arose between them. He had formerly defrauded his guardian out of a considerable sum of money, which was the reason for his lengthy residence in one of the lesser South American republics. During the quarrel he killed his guardian and staged the fake suicide that, but for my intervention, would undoubtedly have succeeded in deceiving the police. Carter then left as he had come, quite unseen. In a hotel as busy as the Regal it would not be difficult for a man to wander about without anyone wondering who he was and what was his business there.'

'As I suggested,' Miss Frayle added.

'As you suggested,' Doctor Morelle

nodded bleakly. 'But he became some-what anxious to know if his deception had succeeded and so he returned to the scene of the crime — '

'And promptly did himself no good,' interposed Miss Frayle.

'Precisely!' said Doctor Morelle. 'What drew my attention to the deception which he was practising was his statement that he had read of his guardian's suicide at the Regal Hotel in the Stop Press column of the lunchtime edition of one of the evening papers. It was obviously false.'

'Why obviously, Doctor?'

'If you had any powers of observation, Miss Frayle, you would realise that newspapers invariably fail to disclose the name of the hotel in such circumstances. This fatal slip immediately proclaimed Carter to be a liar and so aroused my suspicions about him.'

'I see. Quite simple, wasn't it, Doctor?'

'Quite simple. Merely a matter of observation. By the way, Miss Frayle,' he added, 'I was somewhat amused by your ready assumption that the sister of the deceased gentleman was a spinster. You will recall that you addressed her as 'Miss Harrison,' although she had omitted to announce her name. Was that feminine intuition which somehow contrived to inform you that she was not married?'

Miss Frayle smiled. 'No, Doctor,' she said. 'There was no intuition about that — I saw she hadn't got a wedding-ring! Quite simple. Merely a matter of observation.'

6

Miss Frayle Works Late

The usual cause of any disagreement between Doctor Morelle and Miss Frayle was the Doctor's inordinate appetite for work, which resulted in his demanding that Miss Frayle should work for hours at a stretch, and sometimes late into the night.

There was one evening, for example, when Miss Frayle came into the study, having finished a long session of dictation, during which the Doctor had completed his thesis on 'Correlation Factors in Connection with the Determination of Intelligence Quotients.' The thesis had been mathematical in the extreme, and Miss Frayle's brain was swimming. The telephone rang as she entered the study. She lifted the receiver wearily and listened for a moment. Then she smiled sweetly. 'This is Doctor

Morelle's house,' she said. 'No, this is not Doctor Owen's, it's Doctor Morelle's. I'm afraid that you've got the wrong number. I'm so sorry.'

She slammed the receiver down and added, to herself: 'I'm so glad, I mean!'

Doctor Morelle, who had come in unobserved by Miss Frayle, now inquired quietly: 'Might I ask what it is which has induced this feeling of gaiety in you?'

'Oh!' she exclaimed. 'You startled me, Doctor.'

'Not I trust,' returned the Doctor, 'because I have apprehended you in some form of guilty activity.'

'What on earth do you mean?'

'Who was that telephoning?'

'It was only a wrong number.'

'Indeed?'

'You sound very suspicious!' Miss Frayle was beginning to feel the Doctor was being more than usually difficult.

Doctor Morelle smiled. But his smile had in it an infinite suggestion of sarcasm and the most withering contempt.

'Possibly your own conscience prompts that notion in your mind, my dear Miss

Frayle. I suppose it really was a wrong number, and not that you quite deliberately misinformed the caller, in order to avoid any further work tonight? You have been complaining for some time that you have been made to work too late on recent evenings.'

Miss Frayle blushed with indignation. 'Of course it was a wrong number!' she exclaimed. 'I think it is very mean of you, Doctor, to suggest that even if I am dog-tired — which I certainly am — I should so deliberately try to save myself any further bother by — '

Again Doctor Morelle smiled his cynical smile.

'Extraordinarily egotistical you are becoming, Miss Frayle!' he murmured. 'You so constantly take the trouble to remind me of how tired you are! It does not, of course, occur to you that, after several hours of extremely concentrated mental work, I myself might be a trifle fatigued.'

Miss Frayle's eyes opened very wide. This was, indeed, an unusual admission for her employer to make.

'Frankly, such a thought had never come into my head, Doctor,' she said. 'But then, I suppose I don't regard you as quite human. To me you have always been a machine just going on and on like — ' She paused and looked at him in surprise. 'What's that look on your face mean?'

Doctor Morelle replied, in a slightly pained tone: 'Merely that your observation has a strangely reminiscent ring. And one, I must confess, that I did not ever expect to hear from you.'

Miss Frayle smiled slowly. 'Don't tell me,' she said, 'that's what all your other secretaries need to tell you!'

Again the telephone rang and she picked up the receiver.

'Doctor Morelle's house,' she said, and paused. 'Who is that? Did you say Mr. Franklyn's butler? Will you hold on a moment, please?' She handed the receiver to the Doctor. 'A Mr. Franklyn has been found dead. His butler's on the line.'

Doctor Morelle took the receiver and snapped into it: 'This is Doctor Morelle speaking. I see. Very well, I will come along at once.'

He slammed the receiver down and turned to Miss Frayle.

'Miss Frayle,' he began, but she interrupted him wearily, and with a touch of sarcasm almost worthy of the Doctor himself.

'I know, I know! You want your hat, coat, case, and I expect that awful swordstick as well.'

'Really,' replied the Doctor. 'I must admit, my dear Miss Frayle, that sometimes your manner of anticipating my wishes is almost miraculous.'

'Oh,' said Miss Frayle, still very tired, 'all I do know when that beastly 'phone bell rings is to expect the worst will happen — and it usually does.' She made her way to the door, but, before she reached it, the Doctor called after her:

'And, Miss Frayle, we shall require a taxi to take us to Mr. Franklyn's house, which is just off Berkeley Square.'

'Any nightingales, do you think?' Miss Frayle inquired skittishly. But the remark was so sotto voce the Doctor did not hear it.

In a matter of minutes they were

mounting the stairs of a fine, though unpretentious, house in a quiet side street. They were received by a middle-aged man whose skin was a deep brown.

'My name is Franklyn, Doctor Morelle,' he said. 'I have only just come back to this country from the Far East.'

'I had already observed that your features were more deeply tanned than is usual in our somewhat cool climate,' the Doctor replied.

'I wanted to give my brother a surprise. So I thought that I wouldn't let him know that I had returned to England, but would come straight here, without sending any messages in advance.'

'Did you come by ship or by aeroplane?'

'By air. Plane only got in about three hours ago. I reached London, came straight along here, and let myself in with my key. I used to live here, you see. I heard the butler at work in the kitchen, and popped upstairs to my brother's study, where I felt pretty sure he would be working.'

Doctor Morelle said: 'You are sure that

the manservant did not hear you — that he knew nothing of your arrival here?'

'I'm positive,' Franklyn asserted. 'I habitually walk quietly, and I'm certain that he had no idea at all that I had come into the house.'

Doctor Morelle nodded. 'You went to the study, you said, and there — ?'

'I opened the door of my brother's study and saw him leaning over his desk. 'Hello, Harry!' I said. 'Pleasant surprise, I hope.' He didn't answer me, so I thought he'd fallen asleep over his papers. I went over to him, saying something about what a lazy devil he had become. I touched him, and then I realised that — that — '

'And poor Mr. Franklyn was dead,' Miss Frayle murmured, having, in her interest, forgotten that she had been feeling almost exhausted before they had set out on this investigation.

Franklyn nodded heavily. 'At first,' he said, 'I thought it was a heart attack or something. Then I saw the hilt of a knife sticking out of his back. I was going to pull it out. Then I suddenly remembered warnings about fingerprints and the rest, and I thought it would be wiser to leave it where it was.'

'You realised at once that he had been murdered?' Miss Frayle put in; 'I mean, it could not possibly have been suicide?'

Doctor Morelle rounded on her with scathing sarcasm. 'A man would have to perform some rather remarkable contortions in order to stab himself in the back, Miss Frayle!' He turned back to the other to ask: 'And what was your next step, having discovered that your brother had been murdered?'

'My first idea, of course, was to ring for the police,' Franklyn said. 'But I saw that the 'phone wire had been cut, no doubt by the murderer. I rushed downstairs as quickly as I could, shouted for Bates, the butler, and sent him out into the street to find the nearest callbox. What happened after that you already know.'

Doctor Morelle looked around the study in which they were standing. It was a comfortable room, almost entirely lined with books, and a telephone stood on the desk.

'This is the only telephone in the house?'

'Yes,' replied Franklyn. 'It used to be in the hall, but my brother had it moved and brought up here. He had some kink about always liking to answer the 'phone himself.'

Doctor Morelle strode purposefully across the room. 'I observe,' he said, 'that these French windows are not properly fastened.'

'They open on to a balcony overlooking the garden,' Franklyn explained.

Miss Frayle looked at the French windows, her wide-open eyes registering the most complete surprise.

'You think that someone might perhaps have come in that way, Doctor?' she asked.

'There's a lot of old ivy on the wall outside,' Franklyn added. 'A cat burglar or someone like that, accustomed to climbing, wouldn't have had much trouble in getting up to the balcony outside.'

'And poor Mr. Franklyn had his back to the windows, too,' Miss Frayle said.

'He would have known nothing about it, if a burglar climbed up and got in that way.'

The Doctor regarded Miss Frayle with a quizzical eye.

'I am almost inclined to retire and hand over the case to you, my dear Miss Frayle,' he said. 'Your perspicacity is so amazing that I am sure you would be able to solve this little problem without any difficulty at all.'

Miss Frayle looked a trifle alarmed at this suggestion, for while she was ready on occasion to offer ideas, she was under no illusions regarding her ability to cope with a real mystery.

'I think it would be better if you stayed, Doctor!' she smiled.

'If you insist!' the Doctor said. Then, resuming his questioning of the dead man's brother; 'I imagine, perhaps, that a word with the butler might just possibly yield us some worthwhile information.'

'Bates, you mean? I suppose he might have heard something, though he said nothing about it to me. I'll get him for you, anyhow.' He made his way to the door, then turned and said: 'Is there anything else I can do, Doctor?'

'Not for the moment. I may want to ask you some further questions a little later on. You will doubtless remain within call?'

'Yes, yes, of course.' Franklyn opened the door and, turning as he went out, said: 'I'll send Bates up to you straight away, Doctor.'

Miss Frayle and Doctor Morelle were left alone in the room for a moment, then:

'You sent for me, I think, Doctor?' the manservant asked in even tones, as he came in.

'I did,' replied Doctor Morelle. 'There are one or two points which require elucidation, and I think that you might possibly be able to assist us in the matter.'

'Any questions you care to ask me, sir, I shall be pleased to answer to the best of my ability,' the other replied.

'One point has not yet been clarified,' remarked the Doctor. 'When you were sent out to 'phone for a doctor, what made you telephone me? I have never attended Mr. Franklyn.'

'I didn't 'phone you at first, sir. Doctor Owen has always attended Mr. Franklyn when he needed any sort of medical aid, and — '

'Did you say Doctor Owen?' Miss Frayle asked. The man turned to her with a nod. 'But I dialled your number by mistake. I think that it was you who spoke to me, Miss, and told me I had got a wrong number, and it was Doctor Morelle's house that I was speaking to, and not Doctor Owen's.'

'Yes, it was me!' Miss Frayle exclaimed triumphantly. She faced Doctor Morelle. 'Did you hear that, Doctor?'

'I am not aware,' Doctor Morelle snapped, 'that my aural faculties have, during the last few minutes, become impaired.'

Bates was saying: 'I tried Doctor Owen again, but he was out. Then I remembered that my wrong number had been a doctor's number, so I thought that it would be a good idea, since the matter was so urgent, to ring you again and see if you could come along straight away.'

'You telephoned from a public call-box,

I imagine,' Doctor Morelle said.

'Yes. Mr. Franklyn — Mr. David Franklyn, that is — told me to go out and 'phone, since the wires of the 'phone here had been cut.'

Miss Frayle found it impossible to decide just what it was Doctor Morelle was trying to find out — though she had always found his mental processes impossible to follow.

'Have you sent for the police?' he asked Bates.

'No,' Bates replied. 'As you told me you would come along straight away, I didn't think that was necessary.'

'Naturally!' Doctor Morelle murmured smugly. 'I am not unknown in the realm of criminology. And now,' he continued, 'Are you aware if your late employer had any enemies who might be likely either to desire or to engineer his death?'

Bates looked surprised at this question. 'Mr. Harry, sir?' He shook his head decisively. 'Not an enemy in the world. It must have been a burglar who did it. Only a few weeks back we had an attempted burglary. Someone tried to force the front door, and we had all the locks changed, a more modern type put in. There have been several robberies in the neighbourhood lately, too, and I know that Mr. Harry was a bit nervous about them.'

'Anything particularly valuable which he feared might be stolen from the house?' Doctor Morelle asked.

'The house is fairly crammed with valuable stuff left to him when his father died.'

'Mr. Franklyn was a wealthy man, then?'

'I know nothing about that, sir. All I know is that he was always very generous. And you only need to look around the house to see that there was no lack of money.'

The Doctor nodded, then suddenly turned to Miss Frayle. 'Whatever is the matter?' he snapped.

Miss Frayle was looking as if she were scared out of her senses.

'Listen!' she hissed. 'Outside, Doctor Morelle! There is someone outside in the garden.'

Bates turned towards the French

windows. 'Sounds as if they're climbing up to the balcony by the ivy!'

'The same as the murderer!' exclaimed Miss Frayle in hushed tones.

There were now distinct sounds of scraping and heavy breathing, as if someone were climbing up the wall and finding the unaccustomed exercise both difficult and unwelcome. They stood inside the study, rooted to the spot. Miss Frayle and Bates both looked scared. Doctor Morelle silently grasped his swordstick.

'Quiet!' he murmured. 'Don't move, either of you!'

It was doubtful whether either Miss Frayle or Bates would have been able to move had they desired to do so, they both appeared rooted to the spot.

'He's on the balcony now,' Miss Frayle whispered as they heard the sound of footsteps just outside. Then slowly, the window opened, the curtains were pushed on one side, and a helmet appeared, followed by the bulky body of a typical London policeman. He was puffing and blowing as a result of the climb, and he blinked as he emerged into the bright light of the study.

'A policeman!' exclaimed Miss Frayle, her ability for stating the obvious inevitably to the fore.

Doctor Morelle addressed the newcomer. 'I should imagine,' he said quietly, 'that this is a somewhat unusual mode of ingress, officer?'

'I heard voices up here,' the policeman explained, breathing heavily, 'and I saw the window open. I thought it was as well to investigate things a bit. And, judging by what's happening, it seems that I was about right, too.' He nodded towards the inert figure sprawled over the desk.

'I would not wish to dispute that, officer,' said Doctor Morelle.

'Who are you?' the policeman asked.

'I am Doctor Morelle.'

'You are, are you? And what's the meaning of all this?' The other swung his somewhat hostile gaze round the study, and then it rested again on the dead man.

'Who's this?'

'The deceased's name is Franklyn,' Doctor Morelle said.

The policeman shot a suspicious look at the Doctor. 'Know a hell of a lot, don't you?' he said. 'Perhaps you can tell me who did it, Doctor Whatever-your-name-is! Come on, spill the beans, if you know anything about it!'

'As it happens, officer,' Doctor Morelle replied smoothly, 'your appearance on the scene is not altogether inopportune. On this occasion at any rate you will save Miss Frayle, my secretary — ' Miss Frayle for no reason at all blushed a little — 'the trouble of telephoning Scotland Yard.'

'Which will make a change, anyway,' murmured Miss Frayle.

'What's it all about?' grunted the policeman. 'It all looks pretty phoney to me.'

'It is quite simply a case of murder. Fortunately I am able to advise you as to where and how you may apprehend the guilty individual.'

The butler started perceptibly and Miss Frayle clapped her hands together. 'Doctor Morelle! You know who is guilty of killing Mr. Franklyn?'

'But of course, my dear Miss Frayle,'

the Doctor replied. 'In that respect, I do *not* make a change.'

'Of course,' she could not refrain from saying, 'all this is easy as falling off a log, Doctor. But I think that we should all be obliged to you if you could let us know just when and where the criminal made his fatal slip — not to mention that we could bear to have some indication of the identity of the said criminal.'

Doctor Morelle paused to regard his listeners for a moment while he lit a cigarette.

'Yes,' he went on through a cloud of cigarette smoke, 'it was obvious to even the most cretinous intelligence that there was a flaw in certain statements which have been made here this evening.' His gaze shifted from Miss Frayle to Bates.

'Here,' protested Bates, 'are you getting at me, Doctor? I know nothing at all about the murder. I never even knew Mr. Franklyn was dead until his brother shouted for me to go out and 'phone for a doctor and the police.'

'Perhaps,' Doctor Morelle addressed the policeman, 'I should explain to you how I came to be called in to deal with this matter.' And he proceeded to explain how he had received the telephone call telling him of Franklyn's death, and how he had questioned both the dead man's brother and Bates.

He concluded with a brief outline of the course of the cross-examination.

'Now,' he said, 'I trust it will be clear to you whom you are to arrest, and why.'

But the policeman could merely shake his head. 'Don't get it at all, I'm afraid.'

'It is a case which I have seen often paralleled,' the Doctor said, pressing his fingertips together, and once more assuming the pose of the expert instructing students in a lecture room. 'That of the perpetrator of a sordid crime fatally incriminating himself through stupid carelessness, of which he himself is in no way aware. I am quite sure,' he went on smoothly, 'that when you go out into the lounge and arrest the deceased's brother, he will be the most amazed person in the world.'

'The brother!' Miss Frayle gasped.

'Mr. Franklyn's brother!' exclaimed Bates.

'You will recall,' the Doctor continued, 'that he stated he had not seen the deceased for two years, that he had been overseas.'

Miss Frayle nodded vigorously.

'You will doubtless also remember he claimed he had admitted himself to the house with his key, which had remained in his possession from that time, two years ago, when he had left for the East.'

Doctor Morelle's tone took on a note of triumph as he added: 'But how could he have gained admittance as he stated if only a few weeks ago — as Bates, here, told us — all the locks on the doors were changed?'

Miss Frayle gasped: 'Of course!'

'Why that's true!' exclaimed Bates and turned to watch with awe-stricken eyes as the policeman moved swiftly and deliberately to the door to effect the capture of Franklyn's brother.

'And now my dear Miss Frayle,' added Doctor Morelle, 'it is time we made our way home. This case must be noted down while the details are still fresh in my mind.'

'And I thought I was to leave early tonight, Doctor!'

'It *is* early, my dear Miss Frayle.'

'Early?'

The Doctor glanced at his watch. 'To be quite precise, it is just two o'clock!'

7

The Man From Prison

There were occasions when the Doctor allowed himself to become philosophical in Miss Frayle's presence, occasions when she was privileged to hear him give some sort of vocal expression to that materialistic concept of life that he considered to be most closely in accord with the scientific facts as he saw them.

'Yes,' he was declaring on one of these occasions — it was early evening; the study lamp was lit and the curtains drawn as he paced up and down, 'as I dwell upon the complexities of human nature, its magnificence and tawdriness, its wisdom and stupidity I am often led to observe that it is better for the fool to remain within the bounds of honesty. It needs a very wise man indeed to pursue a career of crime with that modicum of success which is necessary to render the whole affair in any way financially lucrative.'

Miss Frayle raised her eyebrows. 'Aren't you sounding a bit cynical, Doctor?'

'Cynicism, my dear Miss Frayle, is a point of view which is arrived at sooner or later by most successful investigators. And you will I think find yourself impelled to agree that I am, with almost monotonous infallibility, successful in those cases which have come under my investigation.'

'Ye-es,' Miss Frayle agreed. But there was a note of scepticism in her voice, which caused Doctor Morelle to regard her with distaste.

'You sound as if you doubt my infallibility in matters of criminal investigation,' he said.

'Goodness, no!' exclaimed Miss Frayle hurriedly. 'It was the genuineness of your cynicism I was doubting.'

'Ha!'

'Even you,' Miss Frayle went on with a smile, 'must have some deep faith in the value of human nature. Otherwise I feel you wouldn't have taken the trouble to help as many people as you do. There is no reason why you should, unless — ' At this point, however, Miss Frayle was summoned to immediate action by the violent ringing of the doorbell.

The Doctor heard the door opening, there was a scuffling sound, a cry from Miss Frayle, and then a woman burst into the study. She was dressed in shabby clothes; nevertheless it was clear that, when less distraught, she was pretty and attractive.

'Who are you?' Doctor Morelle snapped.

'Please help me! Oh, you must help me — !'

Miss Frayle had come in at the woman's heels, and was looking almost as harassed as the other.

'I'm very sorry, Doctor! She slipped past me before I was able to stop her.'

But Doctor Morelle was eyeing the woman, an expression of intense irritation on his face. 'What do you want?' he snapped, 'Kindly attempt to control yourself.'

'Oh, Doctor Morelle! I want your help as I've never wanted anything in my life.'

'I can do nothing to assist you,' the Doctor replied, 'unless you make some sort of attempt to explain who you are, your presence here, and what you require of me.'

'I'm Fred Chappell's wife.' The woman's voice grew steadier and then: 'The police! They've got him, and this time — ' She broke down and sobbed quietly.

Miss Frayle threw a sympathetic glance at the woman then turned to the Doctor. 'You remember Fred Chappell? You found a job for him, about six months ago, when he came out of prison.'

'One of my little experiments in human nature,' the Doctor observed gravely. 'So, my dear Miss Frayle, we are presumably about to have a manifestation of the observations which I was just now making.'

He addressed the woman: 'And what kind of difficulty is your husband in this time?' he asked.

'It's murder!'

'Murder!' gasped Miss Frayle.

'But he never done it! That I'll swear, Doctor. He went straight after you helped him. He was so grateful to you, and he'd do nothing, he said, that would make you think that your help was wasted.'

Doctor Morelle showed no sign of being in any way impressed by these protests.

'Who is the victim?' he asked.

Mrs. Chappell paused before she replied. Then:

'It's old Silverman, the pawnbroker. He was shot dead, and they caught my Fred running away with a gun in his hand. But I know he never done it! You've got to save him, Doctor, you've got to! And you're the only person in the world who can!'

'You live near Euston, don't you?'

The woman nodded. 'And old Silverman's shop is in the next street.'

Miss Frayle said: 'Shall I get a taxi, Doctor?'

'At once,' Doctor Morelle snapped. 'We should, I think, manage to arrive at the scene of the crime before the police, assuming they have reached the scene, finish their investigations.'

The taxi journey did not take them long, and soon they were alighting in a dark, shabby street, running behind Euston station. Miss Frayle thought she had seldom been in a more uninviting neighbourhood.

They made their way past the policeman stationed at the door of the pawnbroker's shop. The officer knew Doctor Morelle and made no effort to bar him or Miss Frayle. The wife of Fred Chappell remained in the hall.

'What the devil — !' exclaimed the burly, square-jawed man who turned on them as they went into the shop. Then he saw who they were.

'Oh, hello, Doctor Morelle! What are you doing here? Good evening, Miss Frayle.'

'Good evening, Inspector Hood.' Miss Frayle replied brightly. She added with a shudder: 'If you can really call it good.'

Inspector Hood nodded grimly. 'I wouldn't look over in that corner, if I were you.'

'In the numerous cases,' the Doctor murmured, 'where Miss Frayle has so very kindly lent her — ah — assistance, she has never succeeded in losing her dislike for the more unpleasant aspects of homicide.'

Miss Frayle shivered. 'I think,' she said, 'it is dreadful such things happen.'

Doctor Morelle made his way across the room to the corner that had been indicated by the Inspector. He bent over the body, examining the wound with care.

'Poor old Silverman,' the Inspector muttered. The door opened, 'And this is his younger brother,' he said, indicating the man who entered. 'This is Doctor Morelle — and Miss Frayle.'

'Yes,' the newcomer said, 'I'm Joe Silverman.' He had a quiet, subdued voice. 'I'm afraid, though,' he went on 'that you've come too late to be able to do anything for my brother.'

'Shot through the head,' Doctor Morelle murmured.

'One shot — but one was enough,' remarked the Inspector. 'However, we've got our man all right. We've got him in the next room.'

Doctor Morelle snapped. 'No doubt you are referring to Fred Chappell.'

'I got here,' cut in Joe Silverman, 'just after it happened.'

'How terrible for you!' exclaimed Miss Frayle.

'Yes, it's a dreadful business altogether. Been staying here for the last couple of months I have, between voyages. Ship's steward, I am. When I'm not at sea, I live with my brother. I didn't see much of him, since I was away so much, but we were always good friends, and this business — well, it's shaken me I can tell you that.'

Doctor Morelle seemed to be in no way impressed by Joe Silverman's interruption. He continued his conversation with Inspector Hood.

'What motive had this man Chappell for committing the murder?'

The Inspector laughed ironically.

'Apart from being caught almost red-handed,' he said, 'Chappell had motive enough, Doctor! It was old Silverman who put in the squeak when Chappell tried to sell him some stuff that he had got from his housebreaking a few months back. That's enough motive, if you like.'

'I am afraid that I'm not entirely familiar with criminal argot,' Doctor Morelle protested. 'May I presume that you mean Silverman informed against the suspect?'

Inspector Hood nodded emphatically. 'I expect that you remember the case.

Chappell got a fairly heavy sentence, but he behaved himself all the time he was in, and he got all possible remissions of that sentence. He came out about six months back.'

'I recall giving him a certain amount of assistance on his release,' the Doctor mused. 'I wonder, Inspector, if I might be permitted to have a word or two with him.'

'Why not, Doctor,' the other shrugged.

'I am grateful to you for your ready co-operation,' the Doctor said somewhat sarcastically. 'And, while I am interrogating Chappell, Miss Frayle will remain here, doubtless to regale you with reminiscences of some of the cases which she has so brilliantly solved — with, of course, my occasional assistance!'

As he went out Doctor Morelle might have heard Miss Frayle say: 'You know, Inspector Hood, I'm a little worried about Doctor Morelle.'

'Worried?' asked the Inspector.

'He's becoming so modest and unassuming that I really think he must be sickening for something serious.'

But Doctor Morelle, however, was out of hearing before Inspector Hood's loud roar of laughter could reach him.

In the next room he found Fred Chappell. The ex-convict was a rough-looking man in early middle-age, and he seemed to be doing his best to ignore the presence of a policeman, who was guarding him. He looked up at Doctor Morelle's entrance. In answer to the Doctor's opening query he answered dispiritedly:

'What's the good of me saying anything about it, Doctor? I been in quod, and that's marked me as far as the cops are concerned. They're only too glad to pick up a chap like me, then they can close the case. I never done it, but I can go on saying so till I'm blue in the face, it won't make no difference to the way things go.'

Doctor Morelle remained totally unimpressed by the other's whining. After a moment he said briskly: 'What was your reason for visiting the deceased this evening?'

'I got a note saying he wanted to see me urgently, at half-past eight tonight. I didn't know what it was all about, but the note made it pretty clear the business was fairly important.'

'Have you the note still in your possession?'

Chappell shook his head. He said, bitterly: 'No. I just tore it up and threw it away.'

'Why?'

Chappell hesitated before replying.

'I didn't want the missus to see it, you understand,' he said finally. 'I was afraid she might think that I was getting in the wrong again. You see, I was tied up with old Silverman in the old days — 'He paused.

'I understand.'

'And I thought that if the wife knew I was in touch with the old geezer again she might think that I was going crooked. But I've gone straight ever since you helped me — I'll swear to that, Doctor, that I will.'

'Did you call here at eight-thirty?' Doctor Morelle queried.

Chappell thought carefully, before replying. 'I don't know the exact time I got here. I told the old woman I was going out for a drink. I didn't want her to know where I was going, like I said. I left home about eight o'clock, I think it was. I walked about for a bit, trying to make up my mind whether I ought to come here or not. I was very doubtful about the whole business.'

Doctor Morelle understood well enough that Chappell would not wish again to involve himself with the fence who had been primarily responsible for his being previously caught and jailed.

'What did you decide in the end?'

'I decided perhaps I'd better call. Old Silverman knew a lot about me, in the old days, and I was afraid he might be thinking of spilling the beans about something what I'd been mixed up in before I went straight.'

Doctor Morelle considered the other's story for a moment.

'And what, when you came into the shop, did you find?' he next asked.

'The door was ajar. I still wasn't sure what was the best thing to do, so I waited about for a minute or two. I listened, but

I couldn't hear a sound. Then I made up my mind and went straight in.'

He paused. Doctor Morelle said: 'Proceed.'

Chappell took a deep breath.

'Well, old Silverman was sitting at the table, with his back to the door.'

'He was alive at that time?'

The other nodded. He looked around, stared at me, and said: 'Blimey! I didn't hear you come in. The door must have been left open!'

'And then?'

'Just then a gun went off behind me and he went down flat. I was all confused for a minute, then I realised someone had shot him and I rushed out and kicked against a gun lying in the hall, picked it up — without thinking — my only idea was to get hold of the killer. Then I dashed full tilt into Joe Silverman, who had just arrived. He grabs me and hollers for the cops. A cop arrives quick — and you know the rest.'

Doctor Morelle stroked his chin thoughtfully. Then he said: 'You were of course, apprehended with the gun in your possession?'

Chappell groaned. 'You said it!' He

went on: 'I never done it, I tell you, but I know when my goose is cooked. I reckon you can't do much for me, Doctor.'

Doctor Morelle made no response for a moment. Then: 'I will ascertain whether or no the Inspector is as sure of his case as he sounds. There may well be a detail that requires elucidation.'

Doctor Morelle made his way back to where Inspector Hood was waiting with Miss Frayle. As he came in he heard Miss Frayle saying 'But of course, Inspector, I spotted the crucial clue right away, told Doctor Morelle, and that was how the thief in that very troublesome case was caught.'

Doctor Morelle gave a little cough.

'Oh!' exclaimed Miss Frayle, and blushed as she realised he had overheard her.

'Well, Doctor?' asked Inspector Hood. 'And what had our friend Chappell got to say?'

'Not unnaturally,' was the suave reply, 'he continues to maintain that he was in no way implicated in the murder.'

'His story is a bit thin, though, Don't you agree?'

Doctor Morelle smiled. 'Doubtless,' he murmured acidly, 'Miss Frayle would detect what she would describe as a crucial flaw in it. Have you ascertained yet the precise time at which the murder was committed?'

'Precisely at eight-twenty-eight.'

'That is precision, indeed!' observed the Doctor.

'Why,' asked Miss Frayle curiously, 'are you so sure about the exact time, Inspector?'

'Joe Silverman here will tell you,' was the other's prompt reply.

Doctor Morelle glanced at Silverman sharply. He said: 'But he was not a witness of his brother's death.'

'No,' Silverman agreed quickly. 'I didn't actually witness the crime. I'd just left the house to keep an appointment. But I heard a shot and sensed something had happened and came running back, just in time to catch that jailbird, Chappell, with the gun in his hand!'

Doctor Morelle's saturnine features took on an even more brooding expression as he said slowly:

'But the time factor. How are you able to state it with such extreme accuracy?' A frosty smile touched the corners of his mouth. 'I presume you didn't happen to glance at your watch just at the moment you heard the shot?'

Silverman shook his head. 'Nothing like that,' he said seriously. 'My watch had stopped, as it happened. I'd noticed that, as I was leaving, and passing a callbox just down the street, I popped in, and dialled TIM. As the voice said 'At the third stroke it will be eight-twenty-eight precisely,' and the first pip went — bang! — I heard the gun go off, and I dashed straight back like I said.'

Inspector Hood spread his hands impressively. 'See what I mean, Doctor? Absolutely open and shut case.'

'It would appear so,' Doctor Morelle agreed — but there was a faint note in his voice which caused Miss Frayle to throw him a quick glance.

The Inspector went on briskly: 'If you're happy about it then, Doctor, I'd better be getting Chappell along without any more delay.'

175

There was a slight pause, then the Doctor said quietly: 'Have you thought that his story may, in fact, be a true version of what actually occurred?'

'But it's only too obvious that he is lying,' Inspector Hood protested. 'He had motive, opportunity, everything.'

'Dismiss him entirely from your mind for the moment,' Doctor Morelle went on imperturbably, 'and ponder on another possible suspect.'

'Who?' asked the Inspector, his features heavy with puzzlement.

'Whom but the deceased's brother himself,' murmured Doctor Morelle.

Inspector Hood tripped up Joe Silverman as that worthy made a dash for it and the cursing, struggling figure was soon overpowered by policemen who came rushing in.

* * *

'I'm glad it wasn't Fred Chappell,' Miss Frayle said a little later. 'It's nice to know you can have some faith in human nature, after all.'

They were back in the familiar study and Doctor Morelle was settling at his desk, preparatory to dictating his notes on the case to Miss Frayle.

She sat opposite to him, her notebook and pencil poised, and a look of perplexity on her features.

Miss Frayle asked:

'I know that Joe Silverman made a full confession to Inspector Hood before we left the shop, Doctor. He was in debt, and knew that he stood to benefit from his brother's will. But how did you ever come to suspect him in the first place. To know that *he* was the murderer, and not Mr. Chappell?'

'I did not *know* anything, my dear Miss Frayle,' Doctor Morelle smiled faintly. 'I simply suspected it, and used psychology. I deliberately waited until Inspector Hood announced that he was about to formally arrest Chappell. At that moment Joe Silverman would have been relieved and elated, believing he was in the clear. So when I told Hood that *he* was the culprit, he panicked, and instinctively tried to make a bolt for it.'

As Miss Frayle looked at him question-ingly, he continued:

'The first point that alerted my suspicions was the fact that Chappell told us that the door was ajar when he arrived at the shop.'

Miss Frayle immediately alerted. She said briskly: 'Nothing strange about that Doctor, surely? Chappell told us that he'd received a note from old Silverman inviting him to the shop at eight-thirty. Since it was after closing time, he'd simply left the door ajar for him to come in.'

Doctor Morelle sighed, and gave his secretary a pitying glance.

'In that case, why, when Chappell entered, was he sitting with his *back* to the door? Surely, if he had been expecting Chappell to arrive, and had left the door ajar, he'd have sat *facing* the door?'

'Oh.' Miss Frayle deflated.

'Furthermore,' Dr. Morelle went on, smiling sardonically at his secretary's evident discomfiture, 'old Silverman was completely surprised by Chappell's arrival. He said, if I remember Chappell's words correctly, 'Blimey! I didn't hear you come in. The door must have been left open.' The clear inference from that was that it was not he who had deliberately left the door open — but someone else. And who was that?'

'Why — why . . . ' Miss Frayle stammered uncertainly, then she brightened. 'Joe Silverman, his brother! He told us that he had just left the house a short time earlier!'

'Precisely, my dear Miss Frayle. He deliberately left the door open to allow Chappell access. Old Silverman, with his back to the door, did not realise it was unlocked. It is unlikely, but not impossible, that Joe Silverman should have simply forgotten to close the door behind him when he left. One improbability is acceptable, but not two.'

'Two improbabilities? What was the second one?'

'The fact that Joe Silverman should have left the house without first ascertaining what time it was. You remember his own testimony, Miss Frayle? He said that he did not think to look at his watch to ascertain the time until *after* he had left the house. Surely anyone leaving to keep an appointment would check the time *before* leaving? How else would they know that they would not be early or late?'

Miss Frayle was still not entirely convinced. 'But what about the fact that he went into that callbox and dialled the Speaking Clock? Why do that if his watch had not stopped, as he said it had?'

Doctor Morelle smiled complacently. 'That was his final piece of elaboration that convinced me of the man's guilt. Only two people knew that Chappell's appointment was for eight-thirty: Chappell himself and the writer of the note. The old man's surprise at Chappell's entrance proved that *he* had not written the note. It had in fact been sent by Joe Silverman in order to bait his trap to frame Chappell, whom he probably knew all about from his brother's reminiscences. He concocted the story of the callbox in order to give himself an alibi for being elsewhere at the time of the shot, and to further implicate Chappell by fixing the time at around eight-thirty.'

'But how can you know that he never actually made the call?' Miss Frayle persisted stubbornly.

Doctor Morelle began to look slightly impatient. 'My *dear* Miss Frayle, if Joe Silverman was so near to the house as to be able to hear the gunshot, why did he need to pay for a telephone call? Why, if he had found his watch had stopped, did he simply not walk the short distance back to the house and ascertain the time there — for free?'

'But your whole case against him was just guesswork, wasn't it?' Miss Frayle said, rallying somewhat.

'Not *just* guesswork, my dear Miss Frayle,' the Doctor murmured. 'When *I* guess, I always guess correctly!'

Miss Frayle gave a long sigh.

'Yes, Doctor Morelle.'

8

The Strangled Film Star

What Miss Frayle found most irritating
about Doctor Morelle was the apparent
absence from his make-up of all trace of
that human quality known as hero-
worship. He might occasionally admire
the work of some colleague in the
scientific world; though even there it
seemed to Miss Frayle that he more often
spent his energies in criticising and
pulling other people's theories to pieces.
But, outside that world, he had apparently, no trace of admiration for anyone.
The film fan, the football fan, the music
fan — he neither understood their
terminologies or their taste. In fact, he
had often remarked to Miss Frayle that
he found the whole idea of admiration for
such people as film stars, sporting
celebrities, or 'best-selling' writers one of
the more nauseating features of our

modern civilisation. In this case, as in so many other cases, Miss Frayle somehow managed to suppress her complete disagreement with the Doctor's point of view. She knew well enough that if she attempted to argue with him on the matter she would be hopelessly defeated in logic, although she knew equally well that her point of view was both a natural one and one which was shared by a fairly large proportion of her contemporaries, whereas the point of view of Doctor Morelle was merely that of those whom she stigmatised in her mind as 'crack-brained intellectuals'.

As has been said, Miss Frayle never let the Doctor have any suspicion of what she really thought on this, as on so many other points, though, now and then she gave herself away, albeit unconsciously when some matter, distantly related to some of her mental heroes or the heroines happened to crop up in the course of ordinary business of her life as the Doctor's secretary.

One evening, for example, the Doctor was dictating to her a lengthy screed on a scientific subject that she found well-nigh incomprehensible. She had several times requested him to repeat a sentence which, while it was doubtless impeccable as to the grammar, was nevertheless exceedingly difficult to understand because of the numerous scientific terms which were bound up in it.

'I'm so sorry, Doctor,' she said, 'but do you think that we could have that sentence once again? I'm not quite sure of what you mean by it.'

The Doctor snorted sarcastically. 'Do you mean to imply, Miss Frayle,' he replied, 'that there is something inherently faulty about my syntax?'

Miss Frayle was not quite sure what syntax was, but she knew, from the expression on the Doctor's face, that to suggest faulty syntax was something in the nature of an insult to the ability of her employer to express himself clearly on a scientific subject. So she hastily disavowed any intention of suggesting any sort of syntactical errors.

'I meant nothing like that, Doctor,' she said. 'What I meant to say was that you used too many scientific terms which I don't understand, and I could not follow the sentence, because I didn't know the meaning of several of the words in it.'

'I do not know that it is altogether necessary for you to explain to me the peculiar workings of what you presumably call your mind,' Doctor Morelle replied. 'And in any event I do not think that it is in any way important for you to understand the exact meaning of everything that is dictated to you, for, if you did, that would mean that you would be on a mental par with myself — and, my dear Miss Frayle, you do not need me to explain that such a thing would be absolutely and totally impossible.'

Miss Frayle smiled. She had heard this retort so many times, and yet she had never succeeded in thinking of the crushing reply that she was sure must exist somewhere, if only she could hit upon it.

On this particular evening, however, she was mercifully spared the trouble of thinking up any sort of reply, for the 'phone rang at the moment when she was faced with the problem.

'Hullo,' said Miss Frayle in her customary unruffled manner, when using the 'phone, 'this is Doctor Morelle's house.'

'Can I speak to Doctor Morelle, please?' said a woman's voice at the other end of the line. It was a voice full of warmth and emotion, and Miss Frayle felt that it was a voice with which she was vaguely familiar, though she could not, for the life of her, say where she had heard it before.

'Who is that?' she asked.

'My name is Carol James,' said the caller.

Miss Frayle was thrilled to the marrow. 'Oh — ' she exclaimed.

'Certainly, Miss James. Hold on a moment, please, and I will see if Doctor Morelle will speak to you without delay.' She turned to the Doctor, and announced: 'Miss Carol James. Doctor, and she wants to speak to you — '

Doctor Morelle sneered. 'By that expression of schoolgirl ecstasy — which is rapidly spreading across your countenance — I should imagine that the name of Carol James has some special significance for you Miss Frayle. Personally, I must admit that I am able, without undue difficulty, to refrain from performing an acrobatic dance at your announcement — '

Miss Frayle's eyes opened wide. She recalled the times that she had sat back in her comfortable seat at the cinema, and had seen that beautiful face, which was Carol James's chief claim to fame, expressing every emotion of which humanity is capable. She had seen Carol James, in 'The Collinson Case,' wrongfully accused of murder, and facing death on the gallows without flinching. She had seen Carol James in 'Orchids and Daffodils' in the guise of an evil flirt, whose machinations led men astray. She had seen Carol James, in 'No Time for Love,' admiring a handsome man from afar, and in the end marrying him, because she had impressed upon him that she was too busy making a career to think of marriage. In fact, Miss Frayle, while not quite the regular twice-a-week film-goer, had gone often enough to be entirely familiar with the faces and the careers of the more famous stars. Doctor Morelle, on the other hand, went to the cinema only to see the more obscure foreign films, French, Italian, and Russian, which he held, were sufficiently adult in their outlook to appeal to the person of sense.

All this had gone through Miss Frayle's mind in a matter of seconds. But, as usual, she did not permit it to be in any way obvious.

She said: 'You *must* know Carol James, Doctor — she's the famous film star. Why, everyone knows all about the time when she — '

Doctor Morelle snapped his interruption of this ecstatic speech, as if he found it almost too irritating for words.

'Kindly ask the celebrated lady precisely what it is that she wants with me,' he demanded.

Miss Frayle again devoted her attention to the telephone. 'Yes, Miss James,' she said. 'I quite understand. But I am afraid that Doctor Morelle is very busy and is engaged at the moment. Do you think that you could give me some idea of what it is that you want, and then I will see if I can get hold of him.'

Miss James sounded very perturbed at this. Her voice shook with genuine emotion as she replied: 'I *must* see him,' she insisted with considerable emphasis. 'He's the only person who can help me. I'm in a dreadful situation. Do you think that he could possibly see me here in my flat tonight? I'm afraid that I have an absolutely splitting headache; otherwise I would risk the effort to come and see him in his house. But as it is I am compelled to ask him to come along and see me.'

Miss Frayle was doubtful at the reception that the Doctor would accord to this suggestion.

'Well,' she said, 'I could ask him whether he would be prepared to come.'

Miss James appeared to think that some more explanation was needed, in order to give a definite impression of the urgency of the matter that was awaiting the Doctor's attention.

'If you can get hold of him,' she said, 'will you tell him that I . . . I think that

I'm in real danger. Someone is coming to see me soon. And I'm desperately afraid of what may happen then, I'm afraid that this will all sound very melodramatic to you, but I assure you that what I am telling you is nothing more than a plain and simple statement of the truth of the situation in which I find myself. Please impress on Doctor Morelle that it is an urgent matter, I'm not in any way a hysterical woman; but I know what the danger is.'

'But, Miss James,' objected Miss Frayle, 'if you're so afraid of someone who is coming to see you, why can't you go out, and so avoid them that way?'

Miss James snapped, as if she was finding her emotions difficult to control: 'I've promised to be here, and I'm going to stick to my word, difficult though it may be. I've got to meet this . . . this person face to face sooner or later. I can't avoid the thing indefinitely. I may as well face it now as in weeks or months ahead. But I do want Doctor Morelle's advice and support, otherwise I do not know what may happen. Do try and persuade

Doctor Morelle to help me. I'm at four hundred and eight, Riverside Court.'

'Riverside Court, four hundred and eight,' Miss Frayle repeated, drawing a pad towards her, and jotting down the address given by Carol James. 'And where is that, Miss James?'

'It's just off Whitehall, towards St. James's Park,' the film star explained.

Miss Frayle's forehead puckered in bewilderment, as if she was not quite sure how she was going to deal with this situation. Indeed, though she had by now made up her mind that Doctor Morelle would have to help this lady in distress, she was not at all sure how that desirable result was to be achieved.

'Very well, Miss James,' she said. 'I will speak to the Doctor about it. I'm sure that he will do his very best to come along and see you tonight, if it is in any way possible.'

'Thank you very much,' said Carol James, and there was a real warmth of pleasure in her voice, which made the conventional words of thanks sound as if they expressed a genuine feeling of gratitude.

As Miss Frayle replaced the telephone receiver she grew suddenly conscious that Doctor Morelle was looking at her with eyes that were grim and menacing.

'Of course, my dear Miss Frayle,' he said, 'I am delighted to hear that you have made an appointment for me at this hour of the evening without even consulting my wishes in the matter; it is, after all, usual for a secretary to ask her employer whether he is likely to be available at the hour at which she makes an appointment for him — or has there been some strange change in the ethics of the profession in the last few hours?'

'But Miss James really sounds as if she needs your help absolutely desperately,' Miss Frayle protested.

'My dear Miss Frayle,' the Doctor said suavely and firmly, 'I can assure you that I have some important matter still awaiting dictation, and that I have no intention whatsoever of leaving my study tonight, no matter how many cinematic ladies may be desirous of obtaining my help because of some awkward situation in which they have succeeded in landing themselves.'

'But Miss James *is* in danger,' Miss Frayle protested. 'I am sure of that, Doctor.'

The Doctor showed the first sign of heat that had been in evidence during the talk. 'I have already informed you that I do not intend to quit this house tonight,' he said angrily. 'And if you imagine that your fantastic delusions can persuade me to do otherwise, then I can tell you, Miss Frayle, that you are making a miscalculation which is as grave as it is stupid.'

To go into details as to the way in which Miss Frayle persuaded Doctor Morelle to change his mind on this matter would be to occupy space which this chronicle cannot afford; it must suffice to say that the methods which she employed will be within the comprehension of all married and most single men. And to add that it was only a matter of half an hour or so before the Doctor, accompanied by Miss Frayle, was making his way across the stone-paved hall of Riverside Court, that massive block of flats near St, James' Park. There was an expression of suppressed delight on Miss

Frayle's face, while the countenance of Doctor Morelle was set and grim, as though he was conscious of the weakness that he had shown in consenting to this visit, which he assured himself was a wild-goose chase.

'Four hundred and eight, Miss James said the flat was, Doctor,' Miss Frayle remarked, as they walked across the hall. 'I think that we had better take the lift, don't you?'

Doctor Morelle looked around him with an air of considerable suspicion.

'The hall porter, whom we should anticipate meeting here,' he said, 'seems to be conspicuous by his absence.'

'Never mind,' Miss Frayle murmured reassuringly, 'we can take ourselves up in the lift, Doctor, I have rung for it, and I think it is coming down now.'

Indeed, the lift slowly came into sight as they were talking, and Miss Frayle, with a slight effort, swung open the gates of the lift. They got in, and Miss Frayle pressed a button.

'Here we are!' she exclaimed brightly. Then she looked around. The lift was still stationary. 'Well, what's the matter with it, Doctor?' she asked. 'I pressed the button all right, and the lift hasn't moved,'

Doctor Morelle snapped, irritable as ever: 'If you care to read the instructions so thoughtfully provided, my dear Miss Frayle,' he said, 'you will observe that it is necessary to close the inner gate before the lift can be expected to perform its no doubt admirable function.'

Miss Frayle regarded the notice hung on the wall of the lift with astigmatic eyes. Then she read aloud: 'Please close inner and outer gates when entering or leaving lift.'

She giggled. 'I am silly, you know,' she said, slamming the gates to.

'That is a remark the truth of which is, I fear, quite indisputable, my dear Miss Frayle,' the Doctor said in his most sarcastic tone.

'There you are!' said Miss Frayle, as the gates engaged. 'But we're still not moving.'

'Press the button again!' muttered Doctor Morelle, his expression that of a man driven almost beyond endurance by the complete stupidity of his companion.

'Oh, yes!' Miss Frayle exclaimed, with another giggle. 'How silly it is of me not to realise how the thing works. It's very simple really, isn't it?'

As the lift ascended majestically to the upper floors Miss Frayle found herself chattering about the woman they were coming to see.

'I'm really quite thrilled to be meeting Carol James, you know, Doctor,' she said. 'She's really one of my favourite film stars. She generally plays slinky, horrid types, who turn out in the end to be innocent. You know, she's awfully attractive, but in a wicked kind of way — if you understand what I mean, Doctor.'

'On the contrary, Miss Frayle,' the Doctor said, 'I am bound to confess that I have considerable difficulty in apprehending you when you talk about these ladies who feature so prominently on the cinematograph screen.'

Miss Frayle grasped his arm spasmodically. 'What was that?' she asked dramatically.

'To what do you refer?' he asked,

'Help! Help!' came a distant voice.

'It sounded to me,' Miss Frayle said, somewhat obviously, 'as if someone was asking for help . . . ' She paused.

'It *is* someone,' Miss Frayle remarked, as the cry was repeated, and nearer now, as the lift slowly moved upwards in the building. 'And it sounds as if it is on the next floor, too, the fourth. Can't you hear the man's voice, Doctor?'

'I can hear it perfectly,' the Doctor said. 'My auditory nerves are in perfect order, my dear Miss Frayle. However, while we remain in this lift, we are helpless to accelerate our progress in any way, I fear.'

Now they heard the man's voice, very much louder than before, shouting: 'Help, somebody!'

Miss Frayle heaved a sigh of relief as the lift drew to a standstill with the curious wheezing sound that lifts customarily give out on such occasions.

'Thank heavens we're here!' she exclaimed.

As they stepped out of the lift, Miss Frayle said: 'Hurry, Doctor, hurry!' But Doctor Morelle seemed to be in no way conscious of the urgency of the occasion, and he followed her slowly as she scurried along the corridor. The man's desperate voice came clearly to them as they emerged.

'It's a man along the corridor,' Miss Frayle exclaimed, with her gift for stating the obvious in a manner that suggested highly original thought.

Now they saw the man. He was glancing up and down the corridor as if he was desperately anxious to see someone who could help him in the dreadful situation in which he found himself.

'I'm afraid you're too late,' he said as they approached.

'Too late?' gasped Miss Frayle.

'Yes, I think that she's dead.'

Miss Frayle's expressive face went pale at this revelation of the way in which violence had suddenly come into the case.

'It's Carol James!' she exclaimed in her most horrified tones.

'I was coming up in the lift,' he explained, 'and I heard her calling for help.'

'Just the same as we heard you,' Miss

Frayle remarked.

'The lift stopped,' the man went on, 'and I rushed out. I saw her struggling with a man just along the corridor here. He saw me, took alarm at the fact that he was being interrupted, and jumped through that window there on to the fire escape outside.'

By the time Doctor Morelle was examining the body of Carol James, which was lying in a corner, Miss Frayle had averted her eyes from the horrid sight.

'She would appear to have been strangled,' he said. 'There are marks of bruising on the neck.'

'I knew that something dreadful was going to happen to her, when I spoke to her on the 'phone,' Miss Frayle said in hushed tones. 'I told you so, didn't I, Doctor.'

'It would appear,' Doctor Morelle said, 'that there is some small foundation, on this occasion, for that feminine intuition to which you have so often laid claim, Miss Frayle,'

'Thank you, Doctor Morelle,' Miss

Frayle said, in tones that expressed gratitude and infinite satisfaction.

The Doctor looked around him. 'I perceive that the outer door of her flat is open,' he said. 'We had better carry her within. It would not be altogether seemly to leave her lying out here in the corridor like this.'

'I'll give you a hand,' the stranger said.

So, between them, they lifted their pitiful burden and got it into the flat, which was furnished in a luxurious fashion. Clearly Miss Carol James had been the sort of person who believed in doing herself well, as far as the merely creature comforts went.

'Here,' said the man whom they had met outside, 'in the bedroom would be the best place, I should think.'

'On the bed,' grunted Doctor Morelle.

'I just wish to examine her for any cause which may in some way have contributed to her death . . . ' the Doctor went on, and the other man looked at him with considerable interest.

'You are a doctor?' he asked.

'I am Doctor Morelle,' replied the Doctor in his most impressive tones.

'Oh.' The man seemed to be quite impressed at this fact. 'I'll leave you with her then,' he said, and made his way to the outer lounge of the flat, off which the bedroom was situated.

Miss Frayle had been waiting there. She had been too disturbed by the events of the evening to take any part in the moving of Miss James, and she had therefore not taken a share in the lifting or the depositing of the actress in the bedroom. Now she looked up in some surprise as the man came back.

'You've left Doctor Morelle in there with her, haven't you?' she said.

'Yes,' the man replied. 'Not that there is anything which he can do about it, I'm afraid.'

'Poor thing,' Miss Frayle said, her customary sympathy with the victim of a crime coming, as usual to the surface. Then she had an idea. 'May I ask just who you are, and how you come to be in this flat?' she asked.

The man hesitated before making any reply. Then he said, slowly: 'I'm her husband.'

Miss Frayle looked more than a little surprised at this. 'I never knew that she was married,' she said.

There was an expression of almost infinite bitterness in the man's face as he replied.

'We separated years ago,' he said. 'She was just beginning to make a name for herself, then. She was only just coming to the fore at the time. That's why we never got a divorce, you see, it would be bad publicity for her, she thought, and I didn't want to mess up her career. But the other day she wrote to me and said that now she did want a divorce, I was coming along to see her, and see if it could be arranged without causing too much trouble. And now it looks as if it won't be necessary.'

There was a tone of desperate sadness in his voice, and Miss Frayle could not suppress her sigh of sympathy.

'And who do you think could have killed her in this dreadful way?' Miss Frayle asked.

'I'm pretty sure I know,' replied the man in a very grim way.

'Who?' Miss Frayle's eyes were wide open as she asked this question, and she pushed back her spectacles, which were in real danger of slipping off the end of her nose.

'Charles Larue,' replied the man.

'Larue?' Miss Frayle repeated.

'Yes; surely you know Charles Larue. You must have heard of him,' the man said.

'The film director?' Miss Frayle queried.

'That's right.'

'He always directed her films,' Miss Frayle said.

'That's right,' replied the man. 'I knew him very well in the old days, but he's been too high and mighty to have anything to do with me lately.'

'Why do you think that he murdered Miss James?' asked Miss Frayle curiously. Even though her sympathetic heart made her feel very sorry for everyone connected with a crime of violence, the long period that she had spent in the service of Doctor Morelle made it totally impossible for her to refrain from asking such questions as would, in her opinion, elicit information likely to lead to a solution of the mystery.

'I don't *think*; I know,' replied the man emphatically.

'How do you know?' Miss Frayle amended her question.

'Because I recognised him. I got a good glimpse of him as he went though the window to the fire escape. I'd swear to him anywhere.'

Miss Frayle was duly impressed by this revelation. 'But why,' she mused, 'should he want to murder Miss James?'

'The answer to that question,' said a sardonic voice behind her, 'will doubtless be vouchsafed to us in the near future.'

Miss Frayle jumped in alarm and glanced around. 'Oh, it's you Doctor,' she exclaimed.

'I am not,' the Doctor replied sarcastically, 'aware that I have an identical twin or other double.'

'Thank goodness!' murmured Miss Frayle in the quietest tones imaginable.

'I am afraid that I failed to catch the exact tenor of that observation, Miss

Frayle,' remarked the Doctor, looking at her in a suspicious manner.

Miss Frayle was embarrassed. Though the remark had escaped her, she had not thought that it was in any way audible to the Doctor, and she was not quite sure what reply would be considered suitable in order to cover her embarrassed feelings. She was fortunately spared the effort of making a reply by the entry of a new character on the scene. They heard a rather rough, cockney voice, from outside the door of the flat saying: 'What's going on up here, eh? Shouting and screaming. This is a respectable block of flats; this isn't somewhere in the Walworth Road. There'll be trouble for somebody if this sort of thing goes on you know.'

Miss Frayle was indeed grateful for the interruption, coming at the moment of her greatest embarrassment.

'That'll be the hall porter, I should think,' she said.

And it was. He was puffing and blowing as he entered, as if he had been indulging in some very unwanted exercise.

'Ah, here you are,' he said as he entered the flat. 'Blimey, those stairs! If I had to climb them very often they'd be the death of me.' He looked around him, as if in considerable surprise at the number of people he found there.

'What's all this?' he asked, and Miss Frayle was hard put to suppress the giggle that rose unbidden to her lips. His words had been so reminiscent of so many stage policemen that she had seen in the course of her career as a playgoer.

'Miss James has been murdered,' Miss Frayle explained, recovering her poise immediately that she remembered the serious background of the case which had brought these incongruous personalities altogether in that room.

'Murdered?' asked the hall porter in amazement. 'Miss James murdered? Who did it?'

But before this question could receive an adequate answer there came another interruption, which made Miss Frayle gasp anew. A tall handsome man of a rather flashy type had strolled into the room unobserved. He too was panting, as if he had been struggling in some great physical effort.

'What's the matter?' asked the newcomer, looking around him in a puzzled manner. 'What's happened? What are all you people doing here in Carol's flat?'

'Larue!' exclaimed Miss James's husband.

'Charles Larue!' exclaimed Miss Frayle, looking at the film director with great interest, not unmixed with apprehension, for she remembered what Carol James's husband had been saying to her a few minutes earlier about recognizing Larue as he left the flat.

'It was him!' exclaimed Carol James's husband, pointing an accusing finger at Larue. 'He killed her; I saw him leaving the building through the window outside.'

'Did what?' asked Larue, clearly puzzled by the course which events were taking. 'What's going on? I don't understand at all! What's the matter?'

The other man glared at Larue aggressively. 'You know well enough what's the matter!' he exclaimed. 'You killed Carol! You devil! I'll choke the life out of you!'

He made a wild spring at Larue's throat, and grappled him, and then, before the onlookers could do anything to prevent what was happening, the two men were struggling together, swaying about the room and overturning tables and chairs in their strenuous efforts.

Miss Frayle stood in a corner, her hand over her mouth and her eyes almost popping out of their sockets. She had seen so many queer and exciting things in the course of her time as Doctor Morelle's secretary that she often thought of herself as hopelessly blasé; but this was almost the first time that she had been the unwilling witness of a fight which appeared likely to lead to serious damage on the part of at any rate one of the participants.

'Oh, Doctor Morelle!' she exclaimed. 'Stop them! They'll hurt each other.' The Doctor smiled sardonically, in spite of the general violence of the situation, for it seemed to him that Miss Frayle's statement definitely erred on the moderate side. The two men were slugging each other desperately. Larue at first had been on the defensive, but he now seemed to be attacking. He had succeeded in pulling the other man's hands away from that desperate grasp on his throat, and he was fighting hard, in the effort to turn the attention of his opponent away from its original murderous intensity.

Doctor Morelle seemed to have little if any desire to stop the fight since he stood by and regarded the two men with quizzical eyes. Miss Frayle found it difficult to believe that he was, in actual fact, not in any way interested in the development of the affair, although she knew that his complete detachment was sometimes what she thought well-nigh inhuman.

'Here, here!' exclaimed the hall porter, who, it appeared, was not as detached in his point of view as was Doctor Morelle. 'Stop that business — one murder's enough for now!'

'He did it — He did it!' exclaimed the man, still clawing wildly in his effort to get hold of Larue's face, and ignoring the blows that Larue was raining on him.

Doctor Morelle at last exercised his

authority. 'Calm yourself.' he said in authoritative tones, grasping the arm of Carol James's husband. 'I fear that your remarks are becoming rather tediously repetitive, especially as we shall very soon be aware of the would-be murderer's identity.'

Miss Frayle looked at the doctor with astonishment writ large on her countenance, '*Would-be* murderer?' she repeated.

'Precisely, my dear Miss Frayle,' replied the Doctor with a smile of complete triumph.

'But what do you mean?' Miss Frayle asked.

'I mean just what I say,' replied the Doctor.

'Do you mean to say,' asked Larue, 'that she isn't dead, in spite of all that this . . . this . . . ' Words appeared to fail him as he indicated the man who had attacked him, 'all that this man said about me just now.'

'I mean precisely that,' the Doctor replied. 'Miss James has now recovered consciousness, and doubtless she will be able, very shortly, to name her assailant.'

'Oh, thank goodness, she isn't dead!' exclaimed Miss Frayle, tears of joy in her eyes.

Doctor Morelle again smiled that

sardonic smile which Miss Frayle knew so well. 'On the contrary, Miss Frayle,' he said, 'it is the victim's well-developed jugular muscles to which thanks are due!'

* ★ ★

Miss Frayle took a long time to forgive Doctor Morelle for having, at this exciting point in the development of the case, told her that she had to go hone, leaving the final denouement to him.

'Why can't I stay, Doctor?' she asked, almost pleadingly, but he was adamant.

'Your presence here is superfluous to the solution of the problem, my dear Miss Frayle,' he said. 'You will hear all about the problem at a future occasion.'

Reluctantly she went, and waited at his house for him to return. She did not have long to wait, since he was with her in less than an hour. She sat there, obediently, with her notebook open and her pencil poised at 'the ready.'

'This devotion to duty is truly touching, my dear Miss Frayle,' Doctor Morelle said as he entered.

'Well, Doctor Morelle,' Miss Frayle said with a smile of welcome. 'I know that you always like to get your impressions of a case down in writing as soon as possible after you have brought it to a satisfactory end.'

'And I imagine that your laudable desire to get my notes done is not altogether unmixed with a desire to know precisely what happened to the fortunate Miss James,' the Doctor added with a chuckle which Miss Frayle thought was positively Satanic.

'Well,' Miss Frayle paused, as if she was not quite sure what was the best answer to that one.

'We will, I think, take that as said, Miss Frayle,' the Doctor added. 'And, meanwhile, I trust that you are ready to take down the notes on the case which I am desirous of getting on paper, as you so sapiently remarked.'

'I'm quite ready, Doctor,' Miss Frayle replied.

'Then perhaps you will take this down. The husband was, of course, the would-be murderer of Carol James.'

'She identified him?'

'She did so; but I had, of course, decided that he was the guilty person long before Miss James was able to accuse him. He had murderously attacked her when she had told him that she intended to divorce him in order to marry Larue.'

'I suppose,' commented Miss Frayle reflectively, 'that she phoned here because of that, knowing the violence of his temper, and guessing that he might attack her when she told him what she was intending to do about the divorce.'

'His story, however,' went on Doctor Morelle, rightly adjudging that these remarks of Miss Frayle's really did not need any comment, 'that he heard her crying for help while he was ascending to her flat by lift, and that he dashed swiftly to her aid, disturbing Larue, who was attacking her, was obviously and palpably false from the start, and its fallacy was extremely easy to detect.'

There was a slight pause, as if Doctor Morelle was gathering his ideas together, in order to go on with his dictation. He cleared his throat, as if preparing to speak again, but said nothing.

'All right, Doctor,' Miss Frayle said. 'Tell me all about it.'

'I was awaiting your cue,' Doctor Morelle said with a sarcastic smile. He went on: 'Obviously the husband would have hurriedly preceded us in the lift which you, a few short seconds later, were able to bring down to the ground floor of the building by the simple expedient of pressing a button there. Had he rushed out as he stated, to rescue his wife from the attack of Larue, he would never have paused to close the door of the lift behind him . . . '

'Of course!' Miss Frayle exclaimed, as if she was just seeing the light for the first time. 'With the door open, that type of lift wouldn't have come for us when I pressed the button, because that's what it said on the notice you made me read.'

'Precisely,' smiled Doctor Morelle. 'And his fatal mistake was emphasised even more by the entry of our friend the hall porter a little later. He, you will recall, had been forced, much against his will and inclination, to climb the stairs because *you* omitted to close the doors of

214

the lift when we hurried out of it in response to the husband's entirely spurious cry for assistance.'

'Well, I like that!' expostulated Miss Frayle in disgust. 'It was *you*, Doctor, who forgot to close the doors of the lift when we hurried out.'

'My dear Miss Frayle,' the Doctor responded, 'I stand corrected. As you say, it must have been I . . . '

'What?' gasped Miss Frayle, in the most complete astonishment. 'You stand corrected, Doctor? Oh, dear, dear.'

'What is the matter now, Miss Frayle?' the Doctor asked.

'I . . . I feel quite faint,' Miss Frayle said.

Doctor Morelle smiled again. 'Naturally, my dear Miss Frayle,' he said, 'I permitted you to precede me out of the lift. However urgent the occasion might be, I should never allow myself to be in any way lacking in courtesy, even to you!'

After that, Miss Frayle no longer felt faint.

THE END

We do hope that you have enjoyed reading this large print book.

Did you know that all of our titles are available for purchase?

We publish a wide range of high quality large print books including:
Romances, Mysteries, Classics
General Fiction
Non Fiction and Westerns

Special interest titles available in large print are:
The Little Oxford Dictionary
Music Book, Song Book
Hymn Book, Service Book

Also available from us courtesy of Oxford University Press:
Young Readers' Dictionary
(large print edition)
Young Readers' Thesaurus
(large print edition)

For further information or a free brochure, please contact us at:
Ulverscroft Large Print Books Ltd.,
The Green, Bradgate Road, Anstey,
Leicester, LE7 7FU, England.
Tel: (00 44) **0116 236 4325**
Fax: (00 44) **0116 234 0205**

CALL IN THE FEDS!

Gordon Landsborough

In Freshwater, Captain Lanny was an honest cop with problems: his men and his chief were on the take from the local gangster Boss Myrtle. Bonnie, Myrtle's daughter, was in love with Lanny, but he couldn't pursue the relationship because of her father's criminal activities. Lanny's problems multiplied as Freshwater became threatened by an influx of murderous criminals from New York — a gang of bank raiders, and Pretty Boy, a psychotic murderer of young women. Then Bonnie went missing . . .

THE EDEN MYSTERY

Sydney J. Bounds

Interstellar entrepreneurs, the Eden clan, had opened up new planets, building a galactic empire, governed by the United Worlds' Federation. However, stability is threatened by an impending war between the worlds of Technos and Mogul. The Federation fears intervention by the clan's sole survivor, Kyle Eden. Meanwhile, Hew Keston is investigating the Eden family's history for the media corporation Stereoscopic Inc. But his life is in danger — someone is stopping him from learning the secrets of the Eden clan!